Rocking Horse Road

Carl Nixon

EasyRead Large

Copyright Page from the Original Book

National Library of New Zealand Cataloguing-in-Publication Data
Nixon, Carl, 1967-
Rocking Horse Road / Carl Nixon.
ISBN 978-186941-907-3
I. Title.
NZ823.2–dc 22

A VINTAGE BOOK
published by
Random House New Zealand
18 Poland Road, Glenfield, Auckland, New Zealand
www.randomhouse.co.nz

Random House International
Random House
20 Vauxhall Bridge Road
London, SW1V 2SA
United Kingdom

Random House Australia (Pty) Ltd
20 Alfred Street, Milsons Point, Sydney,
New South Wales 2061, Australia

Random House South Africa Pty Ltd
Isle of Houghton
Corner Boundary Road and Carse O'Gowrie
Houghton 2198, South Africa

Random House Publishers India Private Ltd
301 World Trade Tower, Hotel Intercontinental Grand Complex,
Barakhamba Lane, New Delhi 110 001, India

First published 2007

Design: Elin Bruhn Termannsen
Cover photograph: Stephanie Nixon
Cover design: Clint Hutzulak / Mutasis Creative
Printed in Australia by Griffin Press

Carl Nixon is a full-time writer of fiction and plays. His first book, *Fish 'n' Chip Shop Song and Other Stories* (Vintage, 2006) was shortlisted for the Commonwealth Writers' Prize in the Best First Book, South East Asia and South Pacific category. Recent works for the stage include adaptations of Lloyd Jones' Deutz Medal winner *The Book of Fame* and J.M. Coetzee's Booker Prize winner *Disgrace.* In 2006 Carl held the Ursula Bethell Residency in Creative Writing at the University of Canterbury (supported by Creative New Zealand). He lives in Christchurch with his young family.

For Rebecca, Alice and Fenton

AUTHOR'S NOTE

While New Brighton and the Spit are real places, their existence in my novel owes as much to my impressions and memories of the area as it does to that suburb's actual geography or history. The people, though—schoolboys, schoolgirls, teachers, parents, Springbok tour supporters and anti-tour marchers—are products of my imagination. They are not based on any real people either living or dead.

This novel was written while I was the Ursula Bethell Creative New Zealand writer in residence at Canterbury University. Without the residency it would not have been completed. Parts of the novel have appeared in *The Press,* January 2007, and in *The Best New Zealand Fiction Volume 3,* edited by Fiona Kidman (Vintage, 2006). My thanks to the following for their support and advice: Professor Patrick Evans, Dr Caroline Foster, Paul Duignan, Gillian Newman of UBS, and Jeffrey Paparoa Holman. And thanks also to my editor Claire Gummer, and my always enthusiastic publisher Harriet Allan.

...you have searched me out and known me:
you know when I sit down and when I stand up,
you discern my thoughts from afar.
You mark my path, and the places where I rest;
You are acquainted with all my ways.

If I take the wings of the dawn
and alight at the uttermost parts of the sea,
even there your hand will lead me
and your right hand will hold me fast.

Psalm 139

ONE

It was Pete Marshall who found Lucy's naked body down on the beach, near the end of Rocking Horse Road. Almost three decades have passed since then, and a whole century has come to a close, but we can still tell you exactly where Lucy was lying. Her body was at the foot of the sand dunes where the high tide had discarded her, close to the sign warning people about tidal rips and swimming near the deep channel that connects the estuary to the ocean and marks the end of the Spit. Right from the very beginning, it was obvious that neither of these mundane dangers had killed Lucy Asher.

It was December the twenty-first, 1980, a Sunday and four days before Christmas. It was half past seven in the morning. The summer was already shaping up to be one of the hottest anyone could remember. The sky was clear and the sand already warm to the touch. That day was always going to be a scorcher.

The dunes were (and still are) criss-crossed with paths both official and improvised, but Pete ignored them all and ran the most direct way back to the road. He stuck to the sandy ridges, leaping hollows and crashing though lupins until, panting like a dog, he arrived at Jase Harbidge's door. Jase's dad was Senior Sergeant Bill Harbidge, who in a few minutes would himself be running behind Pete over the dunes, wearing faded shorts, his shoelaces lashing his ankles and a white shirt, snatched from the clothesline, flapping open around him.

'Like a big white albatross' was how Pete described him, years later. 'I remember him bounding down the face of the last dune and it seemed to me that he might take off into the sky. I guess I was pretty freaked out.'

We have often discussed how there had been an unusually high tide the night before. Not a storm, just a very high tide with larger-than-normal waves. Big swells had barrelled across the southern Pacific in the darkness before rising up and breaking one after another after another against the beach. Each one was ushered in by a stiff easterly wind. In retrospect, it's easy to give events a significance they didn't have at the time but, in the days immediately following the discovery of Lucy's body, several of us recalled lying in our beds and listening to the waves rolling into the beach that night. We had imagined them eating away at the dunes that were the only defence our homes had against the ocean. The wavesound was a dull background roar we had grown up with but, neverthe-less, could not entirely shut out. We could hear it over our teachers' voices as we sat in class, and as we ate our lunches in the sandy grounds of South Brighton High School. The sound rose above the chatter of our brothers and sisters as we ate at our kitchen tables. It was the soundtrack to our awkward adolescence. But to more than one of us, as we lay in our rooms on the night Lucy Asher was murdered, the sound of the waves seemed to have deepened and become mournful. An endless train going by in the darkness, cursed to be always passing, never gone.

Standing in the Harbidges' doorway, Pete told Bill Harbidge that he'd been down on the beach at half past seven that morning walking his dog. It wasn't a very convincing story—for a start, Pete's family didn't own a dog. Later that day, during the official police interview, Pete changed his story. Not that anybody noticed. Pete was not being treated as a suspect. We have a copy of the police report *(Exhibit 2).* Pete claimed, for the record, that he was down on the beach jogging to get fit for the rugby season. At least his revised version of events bore *some* scrutiny. Pete did play for our school's under-sixteen team, although nobody began training that late in the year. It is doubtful whether even an All Black would have been out pounding the sand at half past seven in the morning four days before Christmas.

Pete confessed to us, several days later, that he'd actually been in the dunes retrieving a copy of *Penthouse* he'd pilfered from his older brother (Tony Marshall who would, in a few months' time, join the navy and vanish from the Spit and from our lives). Pete had hidden the magazine—along with half a block of milk chocolate shoplifted from Lucy's parents' dairy, and some suntan oil—in a metal tackle-box he'd buried in a natural amphitheatre in the dunes. The place was surrounded by tall lupins and was almost impossible for the uninitiated to find unless they stumbled across it. Some of us used it as a meeting place, though that morning Pete had been alone.

So why had he gone up to the top of the dunes? When we asked, Pete said he didn't know. He just wanted to look. At the waves? At the risen sun? At the first surfers who, like dark seals, were paddling out to sea up the beach by the surf club? A shrug. Just to look, apparently.

So there's Pete, fifteen, his head full of air-brushed fantasy, walking to the top of the dunes, pushing through the tussock and lupin, and looking out over the deserted beach. The high tide had shifted the sand around, as it always did, so that Pete looked at a landscape subtly changed from the last time he had seen it.

'What did you think she was doing?' (This is from the official police interview now.)

'I thought she was sunbathing.'

'At seven thirty in the morning?'

And then Pete had said something to the inter-viewing officer that showed more insight than most people gave him credit for. 'When you're fifteen and you see a naked girl lying on the beach you stop thinking that clearly. I thought she was sunbathing.'

Lucy lay slightly on her side, her head turned away from him. He could not see her face. He did not recognise her. Her right arm and shoulder were partially buried in the sand, but Pete couldn't see that at first. Her head rested just below the high-tide mark where the darker, waterlogged sand met the dunes with their covering of tussocks and scraggling lupins. Her arms and legs were slightly out from her body—'splayed like a starfish' was how one reporter (inaccurately) described her on the front page of the following morning's *Press.* One leg was slightly further down the beach than the other, extended, as though she had frozen in the act of dipping her toes in to the ocean to test the temperature.

From his vantage point Pete could see her tanned legs, the swell of her hips, and then the rollercoaster dip down to her waist. And, yes, the split and roll of her buttocks which, until that time, Pete had never seen on a real live woman (and still hadn't—technically). And her back. Lucy was a swimmer and a lifesaver and had a broad, lightly freckled back, but Pete had not recognised Lucy's back. Pete still didn't know who he was looking at.

And here we might depart from all the interview notes and official reports to speculate. To Pete Marshall the woman on the beach must have looked like his dreams come true. Anonymous and naked in the stark morning light; a page from one of his brother's magazines brought to life for his own gratification. That idea cannot have been far from his mind (Pete was fifteen, remember). Or, just possibly, he imagined something even more exotic. If, in those first heady moments, Pete Marshall thought of mermaids, or banished daughters of Atlantis, he never let on. Certainly not to the police, and never even to us.

It was only when Pete cautiously moved closer that he saw the naked woman's left arm was strangely mottled. Closer still and he could see that her skin seemed flabby and ill-fitting across her broad swimmer's shoulders. Her hair was matted and there was a bleached finger-bone of driftwood tangled up in it. Lucy Asher had been in the water about five hours before she was washed up, according to the coroner's report *(Exhibit 5).* The body showed evidence of being held down by the waves and banged repeatedly against the bed of the ocean. Pete told the police that when he got even closer he could also see there was something 'weird' about the angle of her head against the sand.

There is one photograph taken by the police photographer *(Exhibit 7)* where you can see a footprint in the sand almost in contact with Lucy's outstretched hand. The hand is lying palm upwards, the fingers slightly curled as though she had been cupping a ball that, sometime during the night, the ocean had prised from her grasp. The footprint is slightly below the body, on the water side, almost touching her little finger. It is from a Converse shoe, the basketball-boot type with a canvas upper that used to come in blue or red with a star on the side over the ankle. We all wore them in those days. All Pete ever said, though, was that he got close enough to see that the woman was Lucy Asher. She was wearing a necklace of bruises, a parting gift from whoever had raped and strangled her in the night, and then tossed her body into the deep water of the channel.

That's when Pete 'freaked out, man' and turned and ran back through the dunes to get Jase Harbidge's dad, who was soon to come flying over the sand like a great white bird.

The Spit is as far south as you can go in the beach suburb of New Brighton without getting your feet wet. It is a long finger of bone-dry sand, only about a kilometre across at its widest point. Down the middle, like a single dark vein, runs Rocking Horse Road. The Spit is the only thing separating thousands of kilometres of cold southern Pacific from the swollen estuary formed by the meeting of the Avon and Heathcote rivers. It is a place with water on three sides, where the tide comes and goes twice a day, and where the sand is always shifting.

In fact the whole of New Brighton is cut off from the rest of the city by water. The Avon River follows the coast before it empties into the estuary and acts as a kind of moat. New Brighton feels separate, like a whole different town. Why bother living down there? That was the general consensus. The city had more accessible and scenic parts than the Spit in which to live. There were plenty of areas that didn't ignore the biblical injunction against building your house on sand. There were always people who muttered darkly about the inevitable tsunami that was only a Chilean earthquake away. The same people talked about how beach erosion could, on a whim, claim back the dunes in less than six months. It was only a matter of time, they said, before all our homes would be washed into the ocean.

It was true that down our way, soil was only a veneer. Tussock and cabbage trees and hardy flaxes were a poor excuse for a garden, but they were all that would grow in sand. And then there was the easterly. That was another reason why most people didn't like the Spit. Most days the easterly wind started up midmorning and blew in cold off the ocean. The easterly drifted salt spray across our homes so that even new cars rusted in a few years. Windows were permanently frosted. When it picked up, the wind blew the sand on the beach at ankle height in a rustling sheet that stung our legs and sandblasted the dunes into soft shapes. It was what the locals called 'the lazy wind'. The joke went that the easterly was too lazy to go around—so it just went straight through you.

New Brighton was a working-class area where people left car bodies and half-built boats out in front of the house for years, as works in progress. Our dads were mechanics and builders, butchers and council workers, and stevedores who worked over at the port. They were the guys who drove the rubbish trucks or built the roads. The practical men who worked with their radios up loud, tuned to the cricket in the summer. Rugby was their winter religion.

Most of our fathers had grown up in New Brighton themselves, and like us thought nothing of the way sand built up in the carpet inside our homes, clogging vacuum cleaners and collecting in the tracks of the aluminium doors. They didn't seem to hear the angry squawk of seagulls perched outside on the washing line, shitting in long white streaks down their wives' sheets. They married either Brighton girls or women who were willing to make allowances.

These days the Spit has turned into desirable real-estate and there's been a lot of infill housing. Most of the big sections have had a drive put down the side, and a townhouse or two built on the back. In 1980, though, there was pretty much just a single row of older houses along both sides of the road, each one with a decent-sized section. The properties on the sea side mostly didn't have fences at the back so that the boundary between the dunes and the sections was purely arbitrary. There were a lot of empty sections too, where weeds and the occasional pine tree grew unchecked and where the rabbit population was kept down by the half-stray cats.

Lucy Asher went to South Brighton High School along with the rest of us, although she was older, seventeen, and had technically finished school three weeks before she died. Her parents' dairy was about three-quarters of the way up Rocking Horse Road, and the Ashers lived in the rooms out the back of the shop. Lucy was the older of two daughters. Her younger sister, Carolyn, was in the year below us at school, in what used to be called the fourth form, but because she was neither attractive nor sporty, Carolyn Asher was all but invisible to us.

Lucy often worked behind the counter at the dairy after school and during weekends. We often went there to get milk and bread and newspapers for our parents. For ourselves we bought small white bags stuffed with chewy milk bottles, Jaffas, aniseed wheels and Eskimo-men. We sucked powdered sherbet through straws and in the summer ordered ice-cream cones, choosing from the eight flavours Mrs Asher stocked. We washed everything down with Coke from glass bottles or, if we were feeling healthy, flavoured milk. We had seen Lucy Asher almost daily, although we had paid her no more attention than the deepening lines on our parents' faces or the colour of the houses we had grown up in. As we came to realise, it is often not until something is gone that you begin to see it.

In the days after Lucy's body was found, the papers were full of the story. Reporters roamed up and down the beach like stray dogs. They stopped us on the road to ask if we had known Lucy and what type of girl she was. Occasionally we would see our own words in the paper attributed to 'a close friend' or 'long-time school-mate of the murdered girl'. Words uttered in passing looked awkward in black and white. They seldom matched what we thought we had said. Certainly the words never came close to describing the Lucy we had seen every day at school and in the dairy.

There was one photograph that *The Press* and the *Evening Star* favoured. It was taken the summer before she died, when Lucy was still in the sixth form. The photo shows Lucy standing outside the surf club holding a small trophy that she has just won for beach racing at the provincial championships. She is wearing the red one-piece togs she competed in and there is a small patch of damp sand clinging to her left shoulder. You can see her from the waist up. She is tanned and smiling and holding the silver trophy out towards the camera with both hands as though offering it up as a gift to the photographer. Her hair is light brown, bleached lighter than it was in winter (we found out later that she squeezed lemon juice into her hair before bed each night in an effort to lighten it). She has brown eyes and a wide, almost American mouth. Though attractive, Lucy was not what people would call a great beauty, at least not until you got to know her.

We still have the trophy, although it was broken later that year, and has never been fixed. About a month after Lucy died it turned up on the street in the Ashers' rubbish. It was sitting on top of the bag and was found by Tug Gardiner who had a paper round that included the Ashers' place. The trophy is actually meant to be awarded for athletics but whoever bought it must have thought it looked right enough for the under-seventeen girls' beach racing:

a silver girl finishing a race, head dipping forward, arms flung backward. The finishing tape is draped across her chest. Apparently the trophy hadn't been significant enough to be engraved with Lucy's name. There was, however, no one else it could have belonged to—and of course it matches the one in the photograph perfectly.

All things considered, it's a very good photo of Lucy. We like to think that in different circumstances she would have been happy for it to be printed so widely.

That summer, the weather had stayed hot right from early November. By the time Lucy Asher was murdered no one was talking about a perfect summer any more; everyone was moaning about the drought. What little lawn there was down the Spit had yellowed and died even before school finished for the year, the dead blades of grass eventually blowing away on the easterly to scatter over the water of the estuary. Only the cabbage trees seemed to thrive. They had predicted the long hot days, flowering in great white sprays in late October. Nearly everything else had the life sucked out of it by the sun.

Except for the sea lettuce: that was also roaring ahead. Whether it was the heat raising the water temperature in the shallow estuary, or the outflow from the oxidation ponds (we called them the poo ponds) that emptied into the estuary at the western end, that year the sea lettuce spread like never before. Lime green, and crinkled at the edges like slippery potato chips, it carpeted the acres of mud that was the estuary at low tide. The sea lettuce threatened to choke even the deepest channels. It sucked the oxygen from the water. Dead flounder and herring could be seen floating on the surface. New warning signs went up warning people not to eat the shellfish.

There were bitter letters to the paper about council mismanagement of the estuary and numerous theories put forward explaining the sea lettuce's sudden bloom. But all we knew was that it stank like nothing else. During the hot days and nights the smell hung low over the Spit. The fug of the estuary at low tide permeated that summer. It was the smell of the rotting sea-lettuce, mud and the dead fish, the flesh of which armies of crabs fought over in the darkness, clicking and clattering. The smell crept into our nostrils as we lay in our beds thinking about Lucy. It got so bad some nights that we could taste it. It put us off our food and stopped us from sleeping.

Some of us took to rubbing Vicks under our nostrils at night. We slept wrapped in the smell of childhood sickness and were taken back to a time when our mothers would tuck us in tight and murmur soothing spells against our fevers. It was a time that, at fifteen, we could remember clearly, but that we didn't yet fully understand was gone forever.

The amount of material we've collected over the years has become a problem. By the time we were in our mid-twenties we already had enough paperwork for two filing cabinets. There are the newspaper and magazine articles, but also the police reports, plus the transcripts of all the interviews (we have the tapes as well). We've kept the larger items: the photograph of Lucy; the trophy of the running girl; the two rafts. There are hundreds of photographs. We've also got a small library on police procedure and forensics. There are books on DNA and fingerprinting. There are lots about famous crimes and how they were solved. Anything really that we've come across over the years that might be of some use or relevance.

Alan Penny was originally in charge of the archives. But Al got married to a local girl when he was only twenty-one and they had three little girls in quick succession (actually, if you do the maths, the first baby came a little too quickly after the wedding). Al's wife told him, when she was pregnant with their third kid, that she didn't want their home cluttered up with all that 'morbid rubbish' so we all came around one Sunday and, under his wife's hard eye, moved the records over to Matt Templeton's place. Matt kept the stuff in a spare room at his house for several years. But when Matt got divorced, the first time, Grant Webb took over for a while.

Most of us have lived with the material for at least a year or two. It's an odd thing to have all that information in your house. You find yourself at three in the morning reading through some article you've read many times before, just looking for a new insight. Or one of your kids will get up in the night for a glass of water and will find you sitting in the dark next to the stereo with your headphones on, re-listening to an interview, the ghosts of the past whispering in your ears. Anyway, it's a fact that having the stuff in the house leaves you bleary eyed and twitchy.

In the end we hired a lock-up. It's a high-ceilinged room with tilt-slab-concrete walls and a roller door, over in the industrial area, past the settling ponds. We chose it mainly because it's only about ten minutes' easy driving from New Brighton, where most of us still find ourselves living. The lock-up is one of about thirty in a compound surrounded by barbed-wire fences, with security gates out the front. We each put in a small amount every month for the rental and we all know the code that opens the gates so that we can get in any time of day or night. Most people use that type of unit to store things like caravans and boats and quad-bikes, or boxes of assorted crap—things that no longer fit into their garages. Ours looks more like a rugby club room. Roy Moynahan is a carpenter now, like his dad was, and he built us a bar out of slabs of macrocarpa. Unlike most of the other units ours has electricity so there's a beer fridge that we keep stocked—although there's always good-natured controversy over what brands we keep in there. There's carpet on the floor over the concrete, and an old pool table. There's even a pretty comfortable bed down the back so that we can sleep over if someone's had a few too many drinks to drive, or a fight with the wife or girlfriend.

And, of course, the files are there. The original material is stored in three tall grey filing cabinets. There is also a large glass display-case for the bigger items, and shelves for the reference books. One whole corner of the room is set up as an office with a computer, which has broadband internet access for doing online research. There's a printer and a high-definition scanner. A lot of the information we've collected over the years has been entered into the computer and stored on laser disks that we keep in a safe in case of a fire. The same goes for the newspaper articles.

The picture of Lucy, the one from the paper, has been blown up and framed. It hangs on the wall near the desk. We like to keep a candle burning on a small table beneath it. It's no big deal if the candle goes out. The next guy to arrive simply relights it.

All in all, the lock-up is a real home away from home.

Even before the ambulance arrived, the two St John's guys breathing hard and moving heavy footed through the sand, locals started drifting across to the beach from their houses. The teenagers were the first on the scene. Perhaps we were more on the lookout for something to lift the morning above the norm, quicker to sense the possibilities. Or maybe our grapevine was just more efficient at carrying the news that there was something out of the ordinary to be seen down on the sand. We called to one another as we came down the tracks through the dunes. But when we caught sight of the body a silence descended over us.

If you believe everyone who claims to have been down on the beach that December morning, there must have been a hundred locals, at least. By our reckoning there were actually nineteen. Roy Moynahan was definitely there, along with Allen Penny and big, lumbering Jim Turner. Grant Webb and Tug Gardiner were there as well. Mark Murray came over the dunes a bit later. He was by himself and his finger-in-the-socket hair seemed to spring up from his head even wilder than normal. Pete Marshall was there too, of course. He stood apart from everyone wearing a mask of sombre authority that none of us had seen on him before, but that he would often put on again during the following months. We stood in a group about ten metres along the beach from the body. We barely spoke. A tight knot of shocked girls hung back higher up, almost in the dunes. The adults who eventually arrived stood in pairs even further back than we were.

The body was being guarded by Bill Harbidge, who had already been back to his house to call both the ambulance and his fellow policemen. He had pulled on his uniform jacket and hat but still had the faded shorts and sandshoes he had been wearing when Pete pounded on his front door. Possibly the shorts were a concession to the mounting heat, but it was more likely he simply couldn't find his trousers in the few minutes he'd allowed himself before rushing back to the crime scene.

The tide that had discarded the body near the foot of the first dune had been full at four in the morning and was well out when we arrived, and the beach seemed very wide. The waves were not as large as they had been in the night but still rolled in with a heavy sibilance. Occasionally one would crash down with particular force and people would look away from the body towards the ocean.

Bill Harbidge announced in a voice loud enough to carry above the sound of the waves that everyone was to keep well back so that we didn't 'infect the crime scene'. He needn't have worried. We would have kept our distance anyway. We were unfamiliar with death and seeing it there on our doorstep in the morning light had unnerved us. Maybe we harboured the primitive belief that whatever had happened to the woman on the beach could be contagious. That, like head lice, death could jump across short distances, from one person to another.

It took us a while to realise who she was. Even over the wavesound, you could hear as the first person spoke her name. 'Lucy Asher.' It wasn't Pete who said it first; he's always been adamant about that. 'It's Lucy Asher.' Who actually said it and exactly how they recognised her, we're not sure. But once those four rolling syllables were loose on the beach they were picked up and passed quickly from person to person. All of the girls started crying.

We tried to recall the last time we had seen Lucy alive. Mark Murray whispered that he had bought a chocolate-dipped double-scoop cone from the Ashers' dairy just the day before. It had been Lucy who rolled it for him. Roy did even better. He claimed to have seen Lucy walking along the road towards the reserve as late as five o'clock the previous day.

It was while we were comparing notes in hushed voices that the two St John's guys turned up, although we had not heard the ambulance. Maybe Bill Harbidge had told them on the phone that there was no hurry and so they hadn't bothered turning the siren on. They came down out of the dunes further up the beach and walked over to the body. They were carrying a stretcher and a large red bag. Bill intercepted them with one hand raised like a traffic cop, which in fact he had been for a few years.

The St John's guy with the ginger moustache seemed to be the leader. He arrived first and spoke to Bill, nodding solemnly. We were too far away to hear what was said. The tall skinny one stood back, holding the stretcher upright in an unwitting parody of the way that surfers held their boards on the beach every day.

When Bill Harbidge eventually stopped talking, Ginger Moustache walked over to the body. Lucy was face down, half on her side. He knelt down and pressed two fingers against her throat. It suddenly occurred to us that maybe she wasn't dead after all. Perhaps by some miracle she was only unconscious. But he shook his head, too quickly it seemed to us for such an important verdict, and moved back to where Bill and his colleague were waiting.

After more talking with Bill Harbidge, during which all three men looked in our direction several times, Ginger Moustache fetched a heavy grey blanket out of their bag and carefully laid it over Lucy's body. After that the two ambulance men looked awkward. They shuffled their feet on the sand and looked up and down the beach as though waiting for a late bus. Their prospective patient was dead. Dead wasn't their field. Effectively they were now like us, just two more rubberneckers.

To us the heavy blanket seemed to emphasise Lucy's death rather than disguise it. To be covered like that, down on the beach on such a hot day, seemed more unnatural than her previous nudity. Rachael White had been in Lucy's class at school, and was the girl crying the loudest even though she had not even been close to being Lucy's friend. At the sight of the blanket she turned her sobs into a plaintive keening that competed with the seagulls' cries. And then she folded up like a deckchair, bending at the knees and waist, collapsing slowly on to the sand. Seeing one of their number fall, the rest of the girls also shifted their cries into a new gear.

It was apparently the tall St John's guy's turn to do something. He didn't seem to be in any particular hurry but ambled over the sand towards Rachael. He kicked experimentally at a lump of rotting kelp with his long legs as he passed, raising a swarm of small insects. He waded into the circle of girls standing around Rachael. Giraffe-like, he spread his feet wide and leaned over her without kneeling, as though he didn't want the knees of his trousers to touch the sand. Some of us also wandered over to where Rachael lay. We pressed close for a better look. But the ambulance guy seemed to have no patience for teenagers. 'Stand back!' he snapped. 'Forfucksake give her some air!'

He produced a small vial from his bag and wafted it under Rachael's nose. She immediately retched back into consciousness. She began crying again like she had never stopped. Two of her friends helped her up and half carried her to a bleached log where she sat sobbing. We all agreed later: it was classic Rachael White. Trust her to shift the focus on to herself at a time when everyone's thoughts should have been with Lucy.

Locals were still appearing over the top of the dunes. Like Chinese whispers, news had travelled fast but not accurately. Some people believed they were coming down to the beach because a surfer had drowned. Others had heard that someone was badly hurt and needed to be lifted through the dunes to the waiting ambulance. Mr Robinson, who was seventy-eight but still swam in the ocean every day, thought he was coming down to the beach to help with a whale stranding. He was carrying a thick O of rope over his shoulder for relaunching the distressed animals. In the event, Mr Robinson's rope would not be required.

It was about half an hour before a dozen uniformed police turned up, along with several plain-clothes detectives. Bill Harbidge looked relieved when the new policemen took control. They herded us further back down the beach and cordoned off a large area around Lucy using long poles pushed into the sand. Yellow tape was strung up between the poles. A policeman was also positioned up at the start of the main track from Rocking Horse Road to stop more people from coming down on to the beach.

Those of us who were there already were allowed to stay. We had nothing else to do so we watched the police work. Canvas screens were put up around the body. We could see the heads of the two forensics guys bobbing up and down behind the flimsy walls like actors in an amateur puppet show. A police photographer was the only other person allowed inside the screens. He snapped photograph after photograph. 'More pictures than a bloody tourist,' was Grant Webb's comment.

Later the police spent several hours scouring the roped-off area for evidence. They moved in a long line, bending to examine the ground every few centimetres. Even the most mundane object was picked up and examined and turned over in the search for clues. It was painstaking work and, frankly, pretty boring to watch.

Roy and Jim did a food run back to Jim's house. They skirted the policeman up on the road and returned with several bottles of Coke, a Boston bun with pink icing and only one slice taken out of it, and some chicken sandwiches Jim's mother had made especially for us. All Jim had told his mum was that we were hanging out at the beach and that we were hungry.

Because it was a Sunday and hot, by mid-morning the beach had began to fill up with families who had come out from town. People mostly parked their cars further north, in the car park up near the surf club where the beach was patrolled and there were flags showing where it was safe to swim. The mums and dads who did drift down the beach soon shied away when they saw the uniforms and the yellow tape. They turned and walked back up the sand with their chilly bins and bundles of beach towels. No doubt they threw an easy excuse to the kids. Nobody wanted to spoil their day by getting too close or by finding out what had actually happened. They'd see it on the *Six O'Clock News* anyway or read about it in the papers over breakfast the next morning. None of the mums and dads was keen to answer the awkward questions the kids would inevitably ask, not on such a gorgeous morning, not so close to Christmas.

It must have been over thirty degrees by lunchtime. The uniformed police took off their jackets and rolled up their sleeves above their elbows. The detectives loosened their ties. No one had thought to bring sunblock: the 'Slip Slop Slap' message was still to come. The policemen's serious faces and the backs of their necks slowly began to turn the colour of cooked crays.

It was Pete Marshall who predicted that the police would not find anything. Pete had drifted across to join us, but he still wore his serious expression. Lucy, he said, was not murdered here – she had only washed up at this spot on the beach. He pointed out to us the position of the body amid the frill of driftwood at the high-tide mark. 'Did you see,' he said, 'the way her arm was buried in the sand?' What the police should be looking for, Pete claimed, was the spot where Lucy had been attacked. We listened to him with a new respect and nodded thoughtfully. Possibly for the first time in his life Pete Marshall found himself cast as an expert.

As it turned out, his analysis was spot on. The police carried away numerous samples in plastic bags. But their forensic work unearthed nothing more incriminating than rubbish that had drifted to shore on the currents from Korean squid boats, and part of a tartan picnic blanket, rotted by the salt water. They also found the partial remains of a previously unidentified species of jellyfish.

We were all interviewed by the police but had nothing to add to the investigation. We were as new to the scene as they were. Only Roy Moynahan's sighting of Lucy late the previous afternoon seemed in any way relevant. A young policeman with scrubbed cheeks, and a moustache that was still thin and patchy, recorded what Roy had to say and then took his phone number and address. But Roy's information must have been deemed unimportant in the bigger picture because no one ever followed up on that first interview.

The police had to work fast because all the tape in the world wouldn't stop the ocean from jostling up the beach. As it was, the waves were only a couple of metres away from reclaiming the body when the two St John's guys (useful again at last) carefully transferred Lucy's body into a black plastic body-bag and then on to a stretcher, on which Lucy Asher eventually left the beach.

We watched them carry her away. Even with two policemen at each end of the stretcher they struggled to keep her level going up the first dune. We said to each other that they were going to drop her. Some- how, though, they didn't. When they got to the start of the boardwalk, the track was easier to navigate and they soon disappeared from view.

We found ourselves alone on the beach. Everything looked the same as it had done all our lives, the beach was as familiar to us as our homes, but we were aware that something had altered, like an only half-sensed swing in the direction of the wind. We gazed uneasily at the cloudless blue sky. We looked up and down the beach, hoping to identify what was different. The air shimmered in the heat.

Suddenly, we didn't know what to say or do. We wandered aimlessly for a while, scanning the ground in imitation of the police. We fantasised about finding some vital clue, freshly washed up, but of course we found nothing of interest. We kicked at the sand, and threw lengths of driftwood into the waves where they were battered in the white foam. But none of our usual distractions or topics of conversation held any interest.

Eventually we drifted back to the road and down to Jim Turner's house. We went there for no reason other than it was the closest. For a while we hung about listlessly on the footpath outside, keeping to the shade of the hedge. On the road the tar-seal was melting. The passing cars made a sound as though they were Velcroed to the road. Small stones rained upwards into their chassis. No one had told Jim's mother about Lucy Asher yet, although by that time word had spread to most of the people living on the Spit. Eventually she came out and fussed us away.

One by one we broke free from the group and returned to our own homes. Daylight-saving meant that it would not be dark for hours. Unusually, we were not hungry, but we knew our mothers would by then have dinner on the stove as they did every night. The uneasy feeling had followed us up from the beach. Now it dogged us, hard on our heels, slipping in behind us through the almost-closed doors of our homes. It trailed around after us all that evening. No matter what we did to distract ourselves we found it there afterwards, waiting patiently.

Finally we grew frustrated. 'Piss off!' we thought, in unconscious imitation of our fathers. 'Getoutahere!'

But it was no good. The feeling was here to stay.

The papers immediately started calling the murderer 'The Christmas Killer'. The stories the reporters wrote in the first few days only confirmed what we already knew. Lucy had been strangled and her body dumped into the water at a different spot from where Pete found her. On Christmas Eve a police spokesman said in veiled terms, at a press conference shown on the *Six O'Clock News,* that the motive for the attack was being treated as sexual. That caused the story to surge back to the front of the next edition of the papers, on the twenty sixth. But as Grant Webb bluntly put it, 'She was naked, wasn't she? Of course it was sexual! He fucked her, then he killed her.' His words made us uneasy, but really you didn't have to be Sherlock Holmes to work that one out. We all knew it right from the start. Lucy's murder oozed sex.

There were nine detectives assigned to the case originally but that number had swelled to twelve by New Year's Eve. There was pressure on the police to catch whoever had killed Lucy. Murders were still unusual back in the early eighties and the killing of an attractive young woman had quickened the national pulse. Of course there was the fact that, like Marilyn Monroe, she was found naked; that didn't hurt public interest or newspaper sales either. Lucy certainly got more coverage than she would have if she'd been a dumpy fifty-five-year-old and fully clothed.

It helped us that Jase Harbidge's dad was a cop. We got first-hand information we wouldn't otherwise have been privy to. Mrs Harbidge had run off with the local butcher six months before so there was just Jase and his eleven-year-old sister and their dad at home that summer. Christmas dinner at the Harbidges' was macaroni cheese, which the three of them ate sitting in front of the television. Bill Harbidge reclined on his La-Z-Boy and downed beers with a steady rhythm. We knew through Jase that he had been drinking a lot since his wife had left. Jase told us that the drinking made him talk about his work, and not just the Asher case. Murders, rapes, gang shootings, the music teacher who interfered with the boy saxophonists, cases dating back through twenty years in the force. The whole works was trotted out by Bill Harbidge. Jase and his little sister sat and ate their macaroni and listened to their father talk. Afterwards they pulled the Christmas crackers Jase had bought to try and make things more festive. Even from the inward-looking world of fifteen we realised that the Christmas of 1980 must have been a pretty strange time for Jase Harbidge.

For the rest of us, our families' holiday rituals started up like well-oiled machines. People seemed to want to put what had happened to 'the poor Asher girl' behind them. On Christmas morning we woke early and unwrapped presents. Later, grandparents were collected from their small units or retirement homes. Then there were more presents, this time of the socks and underpants variety. Then we ate the lunches our mothers had been planning for days. The roast turkey and pork with new spuds by the bucketful was too heavy for such a hot day. We quickly became bloated and slow even as we put away another serving of our mothers' homemade pavlova or trifle. We ate Christmas pudding or Tip Top scooped straight from the tub. On Christmas Day we could get away with stuff like that.

But through all of that, our thoughts drifted towards the body we had seen on the beach. It was disjointing to cast our minds back to that scene while wearing paper party-hats, with mouths full of plum sauce and stuffing. While we were unwrapping our new rugby balls or cricket bats we remembered the way Lucy's head had been pillowed on the sand. And then our thoughts couldn't help twisting sideways to the Ashers. We wondered how *they* were spending Christmas Day. We could not even imagine. None of our parents said anything about Lucy or the Ashers—not in front of us, anyway. Talk of Lucy's murder was conspicuous in most of our homes by its absence.

Only Bill Harbidge raised the subject. The Queen was giving her Christmas message when Jase's dad told him that whoever killed Lucy was smart to dump her body in the ocean. The water flushed away all traces of the killer; no bodily fluids (by which he meant cum) and no fingerprints. Jase's dad also told him, and Jase told us, that Lucy wasn't dead when she went into the water, although the person who strangled her probably thought that she was. Lucy Asher was just unconscious. There was water in her lungs. Technically she had drowned.

We gathered in big Jim Turner's garage in the afternoon of Christmas Day to hear these details. Christmas lunch still sat heavy as a medicine ball in our stomachs. The Turners didn't own a car and they kept an uneven pool table out there. The garage was also used for storing bags of sheep manure, which Jim's dad made him dig into the sandy vegetable garden every autumn. It always carried the musky odour of sheep shit and wool; a smell we eventually came to like. There was a dart board hanging behind the side door and a bench-press with heavy metal plates, which we used to test our manliness while we were waiting for our turn on the table.

That Christmas afternoon the talk was not just of how Lucy died. That day and right up to New Year, the manner of her death became a minor part of our conversations. It was in the Turners' garage that we began to construct our memories of Lucy's life. Roy Moynahan recalled seeing Lucy cut her lip, two years before. We would have been in our first year at high school, form three. Lucy had been drinking from the tap in front of the school library. Some boys had been pushing in the queue and Lucy's face was shunted forward on to the steel tap. Roy told us that he had seen blood flowing freely down Lucy's chin but that she had not cried. For a day or two there was dry blood smeared on the edge of the tap, and then someone washed it away.

Another of us offered up the story of how he had dropped some carefully drawn maps from his social studies folder in the playground. The easterly wind had snatched them away. It had been Lucy Asher and a friend who had helped him get them back.

Lucy Asher riding her bike to school on a rainy day beneath a sky as low as a parking building's concrete ceiling. In memory, the hem of her dress was soaked dark by the water coming up off the road in a hissing arc. The wet material clung to her thighs.

Lucy raising her hand to tell the teacher she had 'women's trouble' and would have to go to see the school nurse. The way the boys in her class had sniggered behind their hands (this was a received memory; one that came to us through Pete's brother, Tony Marshall, who had been in Lucy's class. It was not as authentic or trustworthy as our own memories but was added to our store nonetheless).

Lucy Asher coming second in the intermediate girls' beach racing three years before. We recalled also the feelings, new at the time, that had stirred in us when we witnessed the way the lifesaving girls had begun to fill out their red togs. Over the long winter months, while cocooned inside the heavy layers of their school uniforms, they had metamorphosed into seemingly different creatures.

Lucy, glimpsed from a car window, standing among a group of friends at the bus stop on a Friday afternoon. We speculated that she was on her way into town to see a movie.

Lucy putting up posters of her lost cat, Marmalade, on lampposts up and down Rocking Horse Road. A reward of five dollars was offered.

Lucy and her sister, Carolyn, sunbathing on the wide top step at the school pool. Lucy was lying on her back with her wet hair fanned out around her head to dry on the almost-too-hot concrete.

Lucy Asher playing hockey on a Saturday morning in the sea mist that sometimes covers the whole of New Brighton during spring and autumn. Lucy ghosting up the right wing with the ball. Now seen. Now lost in the shifting walls of mist. Eventually the game had been called off because the mist showed no sign of clearing and it was considered dangerous to carry on.

From that day on the Turners' garage became our meeting place. Most days a few of us would drift in during the late mornings and play doubles and talk about Lucy. Amongst the cicada-click of pool balls and the clang of the metal weights being slid home, with the smell of sheep manure in our nostrils, we gifted memories and half-memories to each other.

Al Penny took to cutting articles out of the paper and sticking them on the unclad wall with drawing pins, next to the photo of Lucy from *The Press.* We read them over and over until our talk became smattered with reporters' phrases. It was not uncommon to hear Pete or Jim or Roy Moynahan refer to the 'profoundly shocked community' or to the police's 'growing frustration'. Perversely, the weather outside was the hottest it had been all summer. The sky was blue and cloudless. The temperatures soared up into the thirties.

Lucy, like all of us, had lived on the Spit her whole life and there was a rich store of small encounters and sightings on which we could draw. It was true that individually none of us could recall that much of her. Because she had been two years older than us she moved outside our sphere. But collectively we had enough grasp on her life to truthfully answer, yes, we had known Lucy Asher.

Lucy's funeral was held in the afternoon on Boxing Day, in the Presbyterian church in South Brighton, only a couple of streets away from our school. The church is a concrete-block building in the shape of a squat cross, with a tower on the front housing a bell that we could all hear from our homes on a Sunday morning. It's a relatively large building dating back to the fifties when attendance at church was all but compulsory. Even so, there wasn't room inside for half the people who turned up to pay their last respects to Lucy Asher. Everyone who lived in New Brighton seemed to be there.

The funeral director must have known his stuff because he'd erected two large cone-shaped speakers above the front door of the church. In the end, about two hundred people had to stand outside and listen to the service through the speakers. The only people allowed inside were relatives and proven friends of either Lucy or her parents. We were just younger boys who lived in the neighbourhood and so we stayed outside in the sun.

A stand of cabbage trees grew in the middle of a yellowed patch of lawn outside the church. Because it was another hot, cloudless day, people tried to position themselves in the narrow bands of shade the trees offered. It was a long service and those who had managed to secure some shade surreptitiously shuffled sideways as the sun moved in the sky, reluctant to give up their slice of cool to the person standing next to them.

We were all there, apart from Al Penny. His parents made a ritual out of setting off before dawn every Boxing Day on their camping holiday to Kaiteriteri. Al had been disappointed that he was going to miss the funeral and had asked us to save him a copy of the order of service to add to our collection of clippings.

The minister's voice came out tinny through the speakers. It sounded as though he was making announcements at the A & P Show. He listed the facts of Lucy's life as though he was talking about a prize calf, but only once mentioned how she had died. Even then he referred only to 'the tragic manner of Lucy's death', and called for a 'prayer for justice but also forgiveness for the undoubtedly tortured soul who is responsible'. That didn't go down well with the people standing outside with us. Dark mutterings rippled through the crowd. Anger shimmered in the air above our heads.

When the minister was through, other people went up to the microphone and spoke, including her uncle, (her mother's brother) and two school friends. Neither girl managed to finish reading out what she had prepared. We shuffled from foot to foot as we listened to their sobs. Through the speakers they sounded like the cries of exotic birds trapped inside the church. Later there were hymns but it felt strange to be standing in the open air singing for something other than a rugby international.

Near the end of the service Pete Marshall did manage to slip into the church, but he soon came back. He told us that he had only made it as far as the rear of the nave where people were standing four deep behind the last pew. From there he had not even been able to see the coffin, and had only glimpsed the minister. Pete's only reliable view had been the back of dark jackets, and the hats of sobbing women, which trembled as though in a strong draught.

Our only sighting of the surviving Ashers was when the coffin was carried out. At the end of the service the people outside divided. We had an idea of how it would have looked seeing Moses part the Red Sea. The people formed a broad avenue from the door of the church to where the hearse had been reversed through the gates. By pure chance we found ourselves on the inner edge of the crowd, with an unobstructed view.

The pallbearers were two uncles and four older male cousins of Lucy's. They all stared straight ahead as they appeared in the doorway. They walked slowly, carrying the coffin at waist height. The Ashers trailed behind: Mr and Mrs Asher in front; Lucy's sister, Carolyn, immediately behind her mother like a shadow.

Mrs Asher looked immaculately groomed, as always. Everyone stared as she appeared at the door of the church. She paused, blinking, at the top of the three concrete steps that led down from the door, and then held up her hands, cupping her face as though trying to stop her features from tumbling down on to the ground. Although she was normally pale, at Lucy's funeral her skin seemed to be actually bloodless. Unless you knew better you would swear Mrs Asher had never in her life left the family dairy, had never before exposed her face to the sun.

In contrast to his pale wife, Mr Asher was tanned a deep brown. While Mrs Asher ran the dairy, he supplemented the family's income with building work—renovations and repairs mostly—much of it done outside. He was a tall, quiet man whose forehead was habitually furrowed. On the rare occasion when we had seen him smile, a slow transformation, like a retreating tide, took place. The high expanse of skin above his eyebrows flattened out and we saw pale lines where the sun had not reached. That day, standing beside his wife, he raised a large hand to shield his eyes from the glare.

As the coffin forged slowly on, Mr and Mrs Asher followed down the steps. They walked between the walls of silent people. Mrs Asher kept staring at the ground, her hands still held up to her face. Mr Asher frowned even deeper than usual. He kept looking above the heads of the crowd as though he had seen something of interest on the horizon; a flock of agitated gulls, or an unusually shaped cloud. Some people in the crowd even turned their heads to follow his gaze. If anything, Mr Asher appeared to be embarrassed by the situation he found himself in.

It was, however, Carolyn Asher who interested us the most. Our eyes were drawn to her. She was certainly never going to be as pretty as Lucy. Later we all agreed on that. Carolyn was pale like her mother, but with large freckles that sat across the bridge of her nose. Looking at her we could tell that Carolyn and the sun didn't get along. She was tall (which she got from her father), too tall really for a girl, if she was going to be considered attractive by boys. Carolyn was flat-chested, with long, skinny legs. 'Lanky' was a word people often used to describe Lucy's little sister.

But as she walked through the crowd that day, following along behind her dead sister and her parents, we couldn't help noticing Carolyn. It was as though we were seeing her for the first time. For one thing she had chosen to wear a black dress too short for mourning. Her thighs were barely larger than her calves but they were clearly visible. She moved like a newborn giraffe coming to terms with height. But mainly we noticed the way she held her chin high and looked boldly at the people around her. It took us a while to realise that she was singling out men for special scrutiny. Men of all ages met her gaze and quickly looked away. Everywhere she looked there was a similar response; it moved from man to man like a ripple through the crowd.

As she passed us, Carolyn met Jim Turner's eyes. Maybe because he was big, she thought he was older than fifteen. Jim managed to hold her gaze for a second and then he too shuffled his feet and looked down. When he looked back, Carolyn's eyes had moved on.

Jim told us, immediately after the funeral, that the look Carolyn had given him had scared him.

'In what way?' we demanded to know.

'It was like electric,' he said, 'like reaching out and grabbing an electric fence.' He paused, sensing our scepticism, and then tried a different tack. 'Or at the zoo, looking at a wild animal, a lion or something in a cage.' He shook his head, aware that as an explanation it was unsatisfying.

'Electric' or not, one thing we all understood about watching Carolyn Asher walking behind her sister's coffin, with her head high and her long pale legs showing beneath her dress, was that it was compelling.

Lucy's coffin was carried to the hearse. The back doors were already open. The three remaining Ashers stood back and watched as the pallbearers placed one end of the coffin gently on to the rollers. There was only the scream of a lone gull circling nearby for accompaniment. The crowd was totally silent. With her uncles and cousins pushing, Lucy's coffin slid smoothly and silently inside the hearse. The undertaker waited for a short while, a few beats that only he could hear, and then closed the doors with a heavy thud.

At fifteen we did not know that there are before and after moments in every life; events people look back on as being gateways into new ways of living, new phases of their lives, sometimes better, but often not as good.

We've all experienced similar moments during the almost thirty years since Lucy's funeral: the ringing phone in the night that signals the death of a parent; the hurled lamp or slammed door that marks the end of a marriage; even something as mundane as an argument with one of our own teenage kids, where things have been said that can never be fully scoured away. Increasingly, the milestones are likely to be medical in origin. A torn hamstring. A ruptured disk that never fully comes right, or the blood test that results in a hurried meeting with a grim GP, and a diagnosis that lands like a slap.

Neither we nor, we now suspect, the Ashers, wanted to acknowledge it at the time, but that short walk from the church to the waiting hearse was a gateway through into a more barren land—and not just for the Ashers, although they were undeniably the worst affected. It was a turning point for all of us living down the Spit. At that moment we moved through to a landscape from which, events would later prove, there was no going back.

TWO

There was a lot of activity at the Ashers' dairy in the days after the funeral. The shop had a closed sign hanging on the door but people came and went from the back of the building in a steady flow from midmorning right up until after dark. Police detectives were the most frequent visitors, as they had been since the morning when Pete discovered Lucy's body. The detectives were usually tall, blocky men in crumpled suits, with an air of purpose about them. There were also relatives who visited, and neighbours. The minister who had taken the funeral dropped by several times during that week, as did the undertaker.

Almost without fail, the visitors would pause with one hand on the latch of the side gate, as though giving themselves a moment to rehearse what they were going to say before they went inside. And then they would push the gate open and go through. Apart from the police and the undertaker, most people arrived with a basket or a plate of food. There was so much food carried inside that we reckoned the Ashers could've lived on muffins and pikelets for a month.

We observed these things from Tug Gardiner's bedroom. His parents' house was almost directly across the road from the dairy. Tug's room was an addition to the house, a boxy weatherboard emplacement grafted on above the lounge. It looked like something that might have been built during the war when people seriously believed that the Japanese were going to land on the beach any day. From Tug's room you could see the ocean to the east and in the other direction we had an unobstructed view of the Ashers' dairy. We reached Tug's room by climbing a set of narrow steps so steep they were almost a ladder. We clambered up like apes, using our hands on the steps above. The room itself was littered with socks and sweatshirts and random clothes that lay where they fell among the tapes, forgotten schoolbooks and scrap paper, the half-eaten sandwiches and wadded tissues—the detritus of Tug's life. We passed no judgement; in fact, we hardly noticed. Tug's room was pretty much interchangeable with any of ours. That included the posters on the walls. Tug's walls were covered with All Blacks. There were the flying wingers, Stu Wilson and Bernie Fraser, and the hard men of the scrum, Haden and Dalton. And of course there were photographs and clippings of the local hero, full-back Robbie Deans.

Watched by our heroes, we looked across at the Ashers' dairy. It was a pretty standard Summerhill stone house but Mr Asher had built an extension right out to the footpath, with large glass windows covered in advertising, and a shop door with a harsh buzzer. The whole front of the place—what must originally have been the lounge and a bedroom—had been turned into the shop. That didn't leave much for the Ashers to live in, just a kitchen and two small bedrooms out the back. We came to realise that as a home the Ashers' dairy was too small for a family of four. Before Lucy died, the Ashers must have been knocking around inside there like pinballs. Most people in the area used the dairy, but even at fifteen we knew that there wasn't a lot of profit to be made selling ten-cent mixtures, newspapers, bottles of milk and bread. Even the popular ice-cream cones were seasonal.

In the slow hot days between Christmas and New Year, and then on into January, we spent our time staring through binoculars across the tar-seal of Rocking Horse Road. The closed sign stayed up and the initial rush of visitors slowed to a trickle and by the second week of January it dried up altogether. By the middle of the month even the police didn't call in on the Ashers any more.

The only person to come and go with any regularity in those days was Mr Asher. He drove off every morning at nine and returned at five-thirty. We didn't know where he went. We wanted to follow him but did not have the means; none of us had a driver's licence. His old ute carried him outside our realm, which extended only as far as our legs or our bicycles could carry us. We assumed, incorrectly as it turned out, that he was leaving to go to whatever job he was working on.

Mrs Asher and Carolyn seldom emerged. They seemed to us to have become like fish in a murky tank, glimpsed only occasionally as they moved in slow sad circles within the gloom. At the time, we thought this was fitting behaviour for people in mourning.

We were not the only people to keep an eye on the Ashers. Rocking Horse Road was a community of curtain twitchers. Lucy's unnatural death was an exotic brush that had painted the whole family. Whenever one of the Ashers appeared, certain people would hover in their front windows and watch. Phone calls were immediately made from house to house, reporting any visible change or anything that could be labelled in the least out of the ordinary.

The only first-hand report we have from inside the Ashers' home in those days following the funeral is from Roy Moynahan *(Transcript: Exhibit 8F)*. Roy's mother and Mrs Asher had belonged to the same Plunket group. Mrs Moynahan insisted that Roy and his eight-year-old sister accompany her, two days after the funeral, to pay their respects to the Ashers.

Roy's mother had to lift the police tape to get to the back door. The yellow tape was wrapped around the whole of the back porch, which gave Roy the impression that the house was a giant present that had been overlooked on Christmas Day. Policemen had been moving around the house since Lucy's body had been found. When the Moynahans arrived, though, the police were on their lunch break. Only one remained; a big man in his early twenties who hovered outside the door and, according to Roy, seemed uncomfortable in his stiff blue shirt and tie.

He asked them the purpose of their visit and recorded Mrs Moynahan's name in a black notebook.

Roy admitted that it was hard for him to get an accurate impression of the inside of the Ashers' house because of all the flowers. They covered every flat surface. In fact there were so many flowers that Mrs Asher had given up putting them in vases. Huge bunches lay on their sides on the kitchen table and on the arms of chairs, across the kitchen bench, and even on the floor in some places. All of them were withering in the heat and giving off their smells in thick waves. Mrs Asher had the windows closed and Roy said the smell and the heat were enough to make him feel sick. Roy and his sister and his mother had to help move flowers to the side so that they could sit down at the kitchen table.

Mrs Asher sat opposite them, stiff-backed, and passed muffins. She wore the same long black skirt and white shirt buttoned at the collar that she had worn at the funeral. Roy said that her long hair was pulled back so tightly from her face that she had a permanent expression of open-eyed amazement. 'She was like one of those people in that movie about the alien body-snatchers. All still and scary.' We knew exactly what he meant.

No one had air conditioning in those days and Roy was wearing his Sunday jacket. The sweat was running in rivulets down his back. His younger sister sat next to him and sniffed. Emma Moynahan had a summer cold but Roy suspected Mrs Asher thought the little girl was sniffling out of sadness, grieving the loss of Lucy.

As his mother talked Roy looked around, trying not to be too obvious. He noticed patches of light grey dust on the edge of the table and over the windowsills as though a large moth had blundered down and flapped around in agitated circles before taking to the air again. It took Roy a while to realise that he was looking at the dust which the police had used to look for fingerprints.

The only showing Lucy's father made was in the photographs hung on the wall behind where Mrs Asher sat. Portraits mostly, the head-and-shoulders type they take at schools every year at the same time as they take the class photos. There were also snapshots deemed good enough to be blown up and put in a frame.

Lucy and Carolyn on a seesaw when Lucy was aged about four and Carolyn just a toddler.

Lucy, down on the beach, grinning at the camera, minus one of her front teeth.

Lucy with one or other of her parents: with her dad and a small black-and-white dog on the beach; her mum and Lucy on the footpath outside the dairy.

There were all sorts of combinations of parents and daughters but Roy could see only one photograph where all four Ashers were together—a formal portrait taken in a park greener than anything the Spit could provide. He guessed that it had been taken quite recently, probably last spring. All the Ashers were posed beneath a large tree. Mr Asher, tall and thin, looked stiff and unlike himself in a suit and tie. Pale Mrs Asher stood on his right, in her usual dark colours. In front of them the two girls sat on a bench. Lucy sat on the left of the picture with her ankles crossed and her arms folded in her lap. Mr Asher draped one protective hand over her shoulder. All of the Ashers were staring earnestly into the camera.

Apart from the dying flowers and the photographs, the other thing that Roy mentioned was the Ashers' Christmas tree. It took up one whole corner of the kitchen, the top pressing hard against the stucco ceiling so that there was no room for an angel or even a Christmas star. As if to make up for this lapse, every other branch was sagging under the weight of the decorations. It was clear to Roy that all the family's presents, including Lucy's, were still sitting beneath it, unopened. By surreptitiously turning his head sideways Roy could read Lucy's name on at least two of the small cards, which still sat on the top of the presents like unbroken pipi shells, mouths partly open.

Roy sat at the table for as long as he could stand it, sweating in the heat, listening to his sister sniffing, and his mother and Mrs Asher talking about things apart from Lucy. At last he asked to use the bathroom. Mrs Asher directed him through a door into a narrow hallway. The toilet was at the far end but Roy nosed around until he found the partly open doorway to what, he guessed, was the room Lucy and her sister shared. Police tape was strung across the doorway. Ducking low, Roy passed inside.

The curtains were drawn and the room was half dark. We can only imagine how Roy must have felt standing there in Lucy's room. Roy had no older sisters and the room must have been a foreign world to him, as exotic and steamy as the jungles of Borneo. He stood inside the doorway, still as a burglar. There were posters on the walls: Sting, Adam and the Ants. A dresser was littered with mysterious tubes and bottles. Roy told us that the smell of soap hung in the air almost thick enough to see. When pressed for further details, he remembered a bunch of dried roses hanging upside down from the ceiling above the dresser. There were also, he claimed, other darker smells he could not identify.

There were dolls, as well. He estimated maybe twenty or so sat piled up on a wooden chest at the foot of one of the two single beds. The dolls made him feel uneasy, as though he were performing to a small, unblinking audience.

Through the walls he could hear the brittle voice of Mrs Asher talking to his mother. Roy walked over and opened Lucy's wardrobe. He imagined Lucy standing where he now stood, selecting the dress she would later be murdered in, holding it up in front of the full-length mirror hung on the inside of the door (would she have chosen a different one if she had known? A stupid question in many ways but the type of thing we used to debate for hours). Roy later said it made him feel privileged to be there, looking at her clothes, breathing in the same scented air as Lucy once breathed.

He was just reaching out a hand to touch Lucy's clothes when there was a cough and Roy realised that he was not alone. Of course, at first, he thought it was Lucy. Who wouldn't? He had invaded her room and now she was there to reprimand him. He spun around and saw a figure lying on the bed beneath the window, on top of the sheets. She was lying perfectly still, staring at the ceiling and with her arms folded across her chest and her toes pointed towards the ceiling. She spoke without looking at him.

'So you found what you're looking for, or what?'

Carolyn Asher was wearing a summer dress that was too big for her. She rose up from the bed and calmly crossed to where Roy was standing. He stood paralysed, wondering how he could explain his invasion to Mrs Asher and his mother. Then, in the semi-darkness of Lucy's room, Carolyn kissed him full on the mouth.

As far as we were aware Roy had never been kissed by a girl, outside of a game of spin-the-bottle at Mark Murray's twelfth birthday party. But if Carolyn Asher was playing a game, she was playing to win. She kissed Roy with an intensity he had only imagined before, mashing her mouth against his. He could feel her teeth push against his lips and then she was forcing her tongue inside his mouth. It was wet and, he told us, surprisingly powerful. Roy was tall and

Carolyn was a year younger but even so she was the same height as him. Roy remembered that she held her body away from his, balancing on the balls of her feet like a ballet dancer. The only thing she touched him with was her mouth.

He didn't know how long she kissed him like that. Suddenly she broke off and stood back, calmly appraising his face. Roy said that her look was definitely questioning, like an artist standing back from an almost-finished painting. Apparently Carolyn Asher was happy with what she saw. He was just about to speak when she slipped past him. She stood in the doorway. 'You shouldn't be in here.' And then she ducked under the police tape and was gone.

Roy stood in the semi-darkness. How confused he must have been. The toothpaste and saliva taste of Carolyn's kiss would still have been on his bruised lips. Lucy's dolls must have seemed to stare at him accusingly. He told us that when he finally left the room there was no sign of Carolyn in the hallway. Disoriented, Roy was temporarily baffled by all the doorways but he got his bearings and found his way back to the kitchen. As he entered the room, for one moment, he imagined that his mother and sister and Mrs Asher were drowning in a sea of flowers, and that only their heads were still visible above the perfumed waves.

During the sweltering week between Christmas and New Year, and then on through the rest of that summer, people took to leaving objects near where

Lucy's body had been found. At first they simply placed their offerings on the sand but the tide and the easterly soon carried them away and so the warning sign became a natural shrine. It was above the high-tide mark and protected from the wind by a dip in the dunes. We never saw anyone coming or going. Bunches of daffodils and lilies seemed miraculously to spring out of the dry sand at the base of the pole before wilting away in an afternoon. Notes and letters, weighted down with hand-painted rocks, would appear overnight. A small brown teddy bear, and later a pink rabbit, lived there for most of January and half of February before moving on.

On New Year's Eve a black-and-white photograph was carefully tied to the pole with a yellow ribbon. It was a picture we had not seen before. Lucy, sitting on a couch, wearing a short summer dress that showed a lot of her legs. She was relaxed and smiling, looking out boldly at the photographer over the top of heart-rimmed sunglasses. To be honest the photo made us anxious. Lucy looked older than we recalled her, more confident and womanly than our memories of her allowed. We were suspicious and jealous of whoever had taken the picture. Al Penny wondered aloud how long would be a decent interval before we could shift it to our files *(Exhibit 14)*.

But people mostly left poems. It seemed to us that everyone who had ever known Lucy became a poet during that summer. They attached poems to the sign with drawing pins and twine but they always blew free. It was not uncommon to find a poem tumbling along the road in the wind or crucified in the branches of a lupin. White poems flew like seagulls against the blue summer sky. They were to be found tossing in the wavefoam or bobbing like small white cradles in the reeds at the edge of the estuary. More often than not the words had sunfaded into nothing or slipped away into the water like fry, but sometimes they could be read.

The consensus among us was that the poems were written by girls. The 'i's were dotted with broken hearts. 'Lucy' rhymed with 'mercy'. Those legible poems we retrieved we felt obliged to take back to the sign. We pinned them back up or weighed them down with rocks so that they would not blow away again too soon. A few of the better ones we took and added to our files *(Exhibit 27 A–F).*

That first New Year's Eve after Lucy was murdered stays with us like a strong aftertaste. Our mood was sombre. Lucy had been dead less than two weeks. We had no desire to mix with the large crowd that gathered every year in the centre of the city to count down to midnight. Although we liked the idea of being kissed by strange women, we doubted we would be the ones bestowed with such random feminine favours. Instead we sought out our own company down on the beach.

Grant Webb supplied the alcohol. It was his father's homemade beer, fermented in the Webbs' garden shed, stacked in rows of recycled brown bottles on shelves from floor to ceiling. As well as lager and stout, Mr Webb made up batches of ginger beer. It was not unusual for the people living in the houses down the reserve end of Rocking Horse Road to hear a dull explosion and know that Grant's dad had got the yeast levels too high in his latest batch.

That evening Grant carried the beer down to the beach in a wooden crate. The sides of the bottles clinked together. He placed the crate in the surf to keep it cool until after dark. We assumed that Mr Webb was not aware that a dozen of his bottles were missing.

We had several hours before one year ticked over into the next and we found ourselves bending to pick up dry driftwood as if a fire had been planned, when in fact nothing had been discussed. We piled the wood at a spot about quarter of the way down the beach. The tide was still going out and would not bother us. The easterly had dropped away as it sometimes did in the evening and the heat of the day had rolled back in over the Spit. Luckily there was still water in the estuary and so the smell of the sea lettuce was not bad. Small bits of driftwood were easy to find where they lay along the high-tide mark and our pile soon grew until it was waist high.

Jim Turner and Jase Harbidge tried to wrestle a sun-bleached log from the sand halfway up the first dune, but it was larger than they had thought and buried deep. We all joined in, digging with our hands, exposing more of the dry wood until it came free. It was dragged over to the pile and dumped on. More sticks were found and several more logs. The heap of driftwood grew and became a pyre that eventually rose above even Jim Turner's head.

When it was almost dark Roy Moynahan used his cigarette lighter on a small pyramid of kindling at the base, into which someone had stuffed some old newspaper. If there had been any wind to speak of, or if we had been less careful in choosing only dry wood, the whole idea would not have worked. As it was, the wood caught surprisingly quickly. The flames soon engulfed the pyramid and, as Roy stepped back, they licked upward. Ten minutes later we had a bonfire that surpassed any of our expectations. It was like a fire you'd see in a movie about castaways; huge and glowing on the beach.

Soon after that, the sun went down behind the long backbone of mountains to the west. Later still, daylight's reflection off the clouds faded from red to pink and then into white before vanishing altogether. Our faces grew flushed with the heat until we had to shuffle backwards to cooler spots.

Grant passed the beer around. The bottles were still wet from the ocean. We took turns using the bottle opener he had initially forgotten and had been forced to go back to retrieve. Jim Turner tried to open a bottle using only his hand. It was a trick he had seen an uncle perform at a wedding but Jim only succeeded in cutting his palm. We had no glasses and drank straight from the bottles. When we put the glass to our mouths we could taste salt. The beer itself had a flavour that surprised us. It was dark and something like liquorice. Whether this was intentional, we didn't know, but we weren't complaining. At the time, we had very little to compare it to. A beer was a beer as far as we were concerned. It was what men drank when they gathered in groups.

We sat on the sand, spread out in a broad crescent with the fire between us and the ocean. There was no wind to stroke up the waves and they were a low murmur, and an occasional flash of white foam in the darkness beyond the edge of the firelight. With the brown bottles in our hands, our thoughts jumped and flickered like the flames but always came back to Lucy.

Mark Murray spoke. His crazy white-boy Afro was a halo in the light from the fire. He did not turn his head but directed his words at the flames as though they were a new type of fuel to be burned along with the driftwood. 'When Lucy was nine or ten...' was how he began.

When she was nine or ten Lucy used to come to his house and play with his older sister. He remembered how the two girls had locked him out of his sister's room, and when he persevered in trying to get inside they had driven him away with shrill, girlish threats. It must have been winter because he recalled that Lucy had been wearing a pink jersey with a picture of a cat knitted on the front.

Someone else chipped in with a memory of Lucy Asher ... on the children's swings, long past when she was a young girl, swinging high, just for the joy of it. She was wearing jeans and swinging her legs forward and back to build up momentum. But what was remembered most was the way she hung at the top of each movement, legs outstretched, head flung back. In memory she was neither moving forward nor going back, but suspended as though undecided.

Someone remembered a day when Lucy was in the playground at school with two or three of her friends. Apparently she was doing nothing much.

Lucy behind the counter of the dairy. There were so many variations on this one memory that they were hard to sort one from another. The time she got Tug Gardiner's change wrong so that she gave him five dollars too much. 'Now I wish I'd told her and given it back,' Tug admitted to no one in particular. Lucy dropping a full bottle of milk that caught the edge of the counter as it fell and shattered on to the lino. Lucy accidentally brushing a sweaty palm with her fingertips as she gave change. Lucy smiling to herself when she thought no one was watching, as though recalling a private joke.

Some of the memories we had heard before; others were new. Before New Year's no one had ever brought up the time Lucy had gone door to door selling Girl Guide biscuits. Now we discovered that this was a memory several of us shared. Lucy had turned up at our doors in the twilight in her blue uniform. Matt Templeton said his family had bought eight packets from her and that his six sisters had scoffed the lot that same evening.

Pete picked up a piece of wood and threw it into the fire. 'I wonder what she would've been doing now.'

We sat silently as, collectively, we tried to imagine. Surely more than one of us conjured up a vision of Lucy, dressed to go out to a New Year's party, seeing the light of our bonfire and coming down to the beach to investigate. She might have chosen to walk barefoot across the sand, her shoes dangling from her hand. It was not beyond possibility. Would she have been alone, or with a couple of friends? Whatever the details, in our imaginations she came forward out of the darkness, not at all shy. After all, Lucy had seen us often at school and we were regular customers in the dairy. We were younger boys and not intimidating. She would have known at least a couple of us by name.

Yes, Lucy would have stayed and talked. Maybe we would have been brave enough to crack a few jokes. Someone would have passed her a beer. Lucy would not have hesitated to sit on the sand and drink with us (we were sorry then that we hadn't thought to bring other, more girlish drinks or even glasses). Matt Templeton was always good at talking to girls. Roy Moynahan could be funny in a not too gross way when he put his mind to it. We could have succeeded in making her laugh.

Someone might have fetched a ghetto-blaster and some tapes from their home so that we would have music. Fire and music and beer. It was not beyond the realms of imagination that we might have taken turns to dance with Lucy Asher, right there on the beach, in the flickering orange light of a fresh new year. And who in our small tribe did not imagine that it was him who succeeded in standing next to her when the countdown to midnight ended?

The beer seemed to have a will of its own. It travelled through us with a determination we had not previously encountered. Matt Templeton was standing in the darkness pissing in a high arc into the tussock for the third time that evening, when Mr Asher surprised him by silently cresting the dune close by. Matt must have been pretty startled because, as he later recounted what he had seen, we noticed that his right foot was wet and caked with sand.

Tall and thin, Mr Asher had stood for a moment in the moonlight. Matt did not think that Mr Asher had seen him. Matt told us later that the light from the fire fell short of where he stood but there was enough light to see the deep furrows on Mr Asher's brow. He was holding something in his hand that Matt described as being 'as big as a chillybin but wrapped in a towel. I didn't get a good look at it, whatever it was.'

Matt stayed perfectly still and watched, but Mr Asher did nothing more than stand and stare across at our fire for a long time. If Mr Asher was aware of

Matt's presence he gave no sign. They were two figures playing stiff candle, in the dark. Eventually, Mr Asher half-walked, half-slid down the dune's face. He began to walk south, down the beach away from our fire. Gulls sleeping on the sand squawked uneasily as Mr Asher approached them in the darkness, but did not take to the air. Curious, Matt followed.

It took Mr Asher about ten minutes to walk all the way to the channel. He seemed to be in no hurry. Matt stayed back close to the dunes where he would not be seen and where the crunch of a half-shell underfoot would not give him away. Eventually Mr Asher stopped near the deep, fast-flowing water. The tide was going out and the estuary was draining quickly. There were whitecaps further out on the water at the sandy bar where the current met the ocean.

Matt watched as Mr Asher unwrapped whatever it was he held in his hand. He crouched down and carefully placed it in the water. All Matt could see from where he was hiding was a slightly darker shape like a small boat on the water. He knew that whatever it was Mr Asher had released would be swept far out into the ocean within minutes on the outgoing current.

Standing and turning quickly, Mr Asher walked away. He had lived all his life on the Spit and even in the darkness was able to walk straight to the start of the track that would take him through the reserve and back to Rocking Horse Road. He passed close enough for Matt to hear his footfalls on the sand and his slightly laboured breath in the darkness. Matt waited for a couple of minutes to be sure that Mr Asher was gone and then hurried over to the water. But he could see nothing unusual. Whatever Mr Asher had put in the channel had been swept away by the current, aided by the slight off-shore breeze, and was long gone.

In the months that followed there were several sightings of Mr Asher in the dunes, always after dark, and nearly always down at the southern end of the Spit by the channel, or moving in that direction. He was often carrying something wrapped in a towel. But that New Year's Eve, in the first hours of 1981, all we knew was what Matt told us he had seen. By the time he returned the fire had died down. We stirred the embers with long sticks and listened to Matt's story. We remembered Mr Asher staring out across the heads of the funeral crowd, seemingly so un-moved. But it was hard to marshal our thoughts. By then it was almost two in the morning and our heads were woolly from the beer and from lack of sleep.

Before we called it a night, Jase Harbidge told us that the vast majority of murder victims knew their attackers. The police, he said, inevitably started their enquiries with the husband or the boyfriend. Or the father. They were, he told us over the embers of the old year, seldom on the wrong track.

So who killed Lucy Asher? That was the six-million-dollar question. That question was like a blowfly in our ears all that summer. It annoyed us with its incessant buzz throughout our waking hours. Like some research essay for English we went over the Ws. *Who? What? Why?* And really, the police didn't even know *Where?* Pete had been right when he said Lucy was not murdered on the beach, not where he found her, anyway. According to Jase Harbidge's father the police still hadn't discovered where Lucy was attacked, or where she entered the water, although they suspected both events occurred somewhere near the channel.

Al Penny was champion of the lone-wolf theory. According to Al, Lucy had probably gone for a walk along the beach and simply been attacked by a complete stranger; an opportunist who seized his moment. 'Someone strong enough to keep her quiet,' he reasoned.

We could not discount Al's theory, but most of us believed that the murderer was someone who lived in the area. We imagined a man, or older boy, who had seen Lucy regularly as she worked behind the counter of the dairy. Someone whose attraction had secretly spawned darker feelings. Her killer was probably someone who she knew by name.

If we are being totally honest, the certainty that the murderer knew Lucy really came because we were able to look into ourselves. We saw the darker side of what it meant to be a man. At fifteen we were full to bursting with frustrated lust. We joke about it now and, after a beer or three, wryly confess to relieving our tension up to twice, or even three times a day back then. It is a stamina we wish we had now. We had also known our share of violence, most of it on the rugby field, but nearly all of us had been in a fight or two off the field as well. Roy Moynahan once took a softball bat to the head of a guy he thought was picking on Emma, his younger sister. It was just good luck he didn't kill the guy.

So really it was not impossible for us to conjure up an image of some man, with feelings similar to those we had experienced ourselves, going out of his way to see Lucy in the dairy. Maybe he followed her home from school a couple of times. Surely not much harm in that. It also wasn't so hard for us to imagine those same feelings eventually swamping a man and driving him to terrible deeds. It's not that we could imagine ourselves raping or killing a woman. The action was fundamentally abhorrent. But let's just say, in the name of truth, that at fifteen we could stand at the beginning of the path that Lucy's murderer must surely have walked down. We could loiter at the start of that shadowy way and see as far as the first bend among the trees. We had an idea what it would feel like to walk down that path ourselves for at least a while.

We looked at the faces of the men and older boys we saw on the street and on the beach. No one was innocent in our imaginations. Was it him? we wondered. Or him? Him? Or him? But because we didn't have any plausible alternative Mr Asher remained our prime suspect. Jase Harbidge had done some research and could trot out the names of fathers (and even a few mothers) who had murdered their kids in all sorts of gruesome ways. Admittedly the cases, like our favourite TV shows, were mostly from the States, but that wasn't to say it hadn't happened closer to home. Sitting around our dinner tables in the evenings with our families, we examined the faces of our own fathers and mothers in a new and disturbing light.

Mr Asher was the only person we knew on whose behaviour we could pin the tag 'suspicious'. We speculated endlessly about what it was that Matt had seen him throwing into the channel in the middle of the night. Possibly some object or piece of clothing that would incriminate him in Lucy's murder? That's the direction our talk swung around to. Mr Asher's habitual silence now seemed to us to be a form of camouflage, allowing him to move unnoticed and unsuspected.

When the idea first surfaced Al Penny had tried to argue. 'But what about the sex? Lucy was raped, right? Fathers don't do that to their daughters.'

It was another hot afternoon and we were meeting in the Turners' garage with its bench-press and wonky pool table. Jase Harbidge was lining up his shot. He paused and looked across the green felt at Al and raised his eyebrows in a way that showed that he couldn't believe what he was hearing. 'Wanna bet?' was all he said. And then he took his shot. The weights hovered in the air and the balls bounced off the cushion and eventually came to rest while we all thought about the unthinkable.

We received our School Certificate results in the mail on the Monday of the third week of 1981. Our marks were average, which is exactly what we had expected. We scraped through into sixth form and avoided the shame of having to repeat the fifth form. Only Al Penny's marks were outstanding. They were so good that he became uncharacteristically cagey when asked how he had done and would not show anyone the official form. On the same day the Asher's dairy opened again. We felt that opening up for business was somehow disloyal to Lucy's memory, but as Roy Moynahan, who was always the pragmatist of the group, said, 'The Ashers have gotta make a living, don't they? Just like everyone else.'

But by then it wasn't much of a living. Business was noticeably slow. People suddenly seemed to prefer to go the extra distance to the dairy up on Bridge Street. It had recently changed hands and smelt of incense and curry (what dairy doesn't these days? But back then it was an alien scent and off-putting for many people). A lot of our mothers started doing the whole week's shopping at the supermarket in New Brighton Mall so that there was no need to top up at the Ashers' shop.

We, on the other hand, became the Ashers' best customers. Our motivation for shopping at their dairy wasn't entirely to do with furthering what we now thought of as our investigation into Lucy's murder.

We genuinely felt that we should help prop up their business. The spell of hot weather was still unbroken so, of course, we bought ice creams. We sat around in Tug's bedroom taking turns with the binoculars and eating. For a while, we each got through three or four cones a day. In addition to ice cream we spent our money on bottles of Coke, Fanta and Mello Yello. Later we moved on to twenty-and fifty-cent mixtures until we grew sick of the sight of pink and yellow Eskimo-men and chewy milk-bottles. As the weeks passed we also came to loathe coiled liquorice straps. We left them to lie around Tug's room like the charred remains of garden snails. We took to tipping bags of powdered sherbet down the Gardiners' toilet.

Our mothers were at first surprised, and then suspicious of the unexplained bottles of milk we began to bring home on a daily basis. We drank all we could but there's only so much milk you can stomach. When we didn't want to answer any more of our mothers' questions, the milk also got poured away. For weeks the Gardiners' drains ran white.

We also bought bread but there's only so much of that you can eat as well. We Frisbeed whole loaves of sliced bread, piece by piece, out Tug's window for the seagulls to catch on the wing. By the end of January the birds swarmed around the house as thick as flies. They perched on the edge of the fences and up on the spouting, just waiting, staining everything with long white streaks. Eventually Mr Gardiner stormed up the stairs and laid down the law.

When we made our purchases, it was always Mrs Asher who served us. Mrs Asher had never dressed like someone who worked in a dairy. She habitually wore fashionable black dresses and skirts and silver bracelets (what we used to call bangles). Her hair was long, like Lucy's and with the same sheen, and she wore it in a ponytail. Mrs Asher dressed as though she had just stepped out of a business meeting at Tip Top in order to scoop out our double ice creams.

We knew that our mothers often used to talk to each other about Mrs Asher and what they called 'her pretensions'. Down Rocking Horse Road, being seen to step outside the carefully pegged-out boundaries of your life was regarded as something of a sin.

But grief had diminished Mrs Asher. It had taken the flesh from her cheeks so that the bones of her face were thrust forward like scaffolding from beneath her skin. She had always been slim but Lucy's death had made coat-hangers of Mrs Asher's shoulders. Her eyes seemed to float in their sockets as she regarded us from behind the increasingly dusty glass counter, beneath which the sweets sat like something in an abandoned museum. The large front windows were covered with advertising that was sellotaped to the inside of the glass. The advertising, for things like dog roll and pies, let through virtually no sunlight. It was always a shock to move from the glare of the hot day into the cool dark shop and it was inevitably sobering. We tried to be cheery but it was an effort. More often than not Mrs Asher had forgotten to turn on the fluorescent lights. The door buzzer would sound and she would appear from the back, silent and pale in the gloom, thinner by the day. She would not speak, not even 'hello' or 'good afternoon', but would stand patiently behind the counter in the quarter-light and wait for us to tell her what we wanted. When we finally made up our minds she would hand it over without a word and we would pay and leave.

It's hard to remember exactly what we hoped to learn by going there. Perhaps we went because it was all in such stark contrast to the way the shop had been when Lucy was alive. The very differences served as reminders and moored us to the recent past. Lucy had served in the shop most days after school as well as on Saturday afternoons after she had played netball or hockey. Back then, the door was always jammed open with a small triangle of wood. There had been light and Lucy's music played quietly from a tape deck that she kept high up on a shelf behind the counter. When her parents weren't home she would turn the music up loud. Lucy was often talking to her friends on the phone as she served, cupping the receiver under her chin and still talking and laughing as she gave change. She was always friendly, even to us younger boys.

Perhaps the truth is that we went to the dairy in the weeks following the funeral because we wanted to share our grief with Mrs Asher. We had neither the courage or the vocabulary to put how we felt into words. Maybe our daily purchases of unwanted ice-cream and milk and sweets were the only form of consolation we knew how to offer.

By mid-January we had started hearing things about Carolyn Asher. They were just vague rumours at first, ripples from a distant splash. And then Matt Templeton saw her on a Friday night, standing outside the fish 'n' chip shop up on Estuary Road. According to Matt she was with an older guy, a local, who had been flanker in the first XV at school but who now played for University. 'The guy was all over her' was Matt's comment.

Tug saw her as well, a couple of weeks later. She was in the back of a car parked outside the reserve, in the pool of shadow between the street-lights. She was with a guy as well, but not the rugby player. It was a surfer this time. She was sitting up in the back seat, smoking. The surfer was back there with her. As Tug passed Carolyn turned her head and looked at him without any expression.

By the end of the month we had heard other, more specific things, told third and fourth hand. By then they were stories told with a wink and a sneer.

The guys Carolyn Asher was seeing were always older and always lived in New Brighton. Because she was Lucy's sister we tried to find out more. We thought our best bet was to approach the guys directly.

'Whatareya, her brother?' was a fairly typical comment. That from a guy who later threatened to beat up Jase Harbidge if he didn't stop hanging around his flat. Really, we couldn't blame the guy for being edgy. Carolyn Asher was underage by more than a year.

Years later we were able to strike up conversations with these old boyfriends in pubs. We would arrange a chance meeting and then simply drop her name into the conversation. 'She was up for it any time,' one guy told us. Another said with a sneer that 'She was a weird little chick, but she did love to fuck!'

Her pattern was always the same—none of the guys lasted very long. Several of them already had girlfriends but, as far as we know, once she set her sights on a guy she never got turned down. After seeing a guy for a couple of weeks she simply stopped coming around. Most seemed to shrug and accept it; they didn't take it personally. They were grateful for the easy sex while it lasted and philosophical when it dried up.

A few, though, seemed to fall for Carolyn. They made the mistake of trying to see her again once she had made it clear it was over. If they called her on the phone or stopped her on the street she acted as though she didn't know them from Adam. One of the persistent ones told us, only a couple of years ago, 'I only went out with her for like a week, but she was an addiction. Even now, seeing a girl who looks a bit like her makes me hard as a plank.'

We were so fixated on Lucy during the days that it was only natural our sleeping selves also began to focus on her. We didn't talk about it with each other that much back then (and didn't later for many years). At the time, we just acknowledged that there were dreams. Pete Marshall admitted to being freaked out by them sometimes ('freaked out' would remain one of Pete's favourite expressions right into his late twenties). It was only very recently that we discussed the dreams. As it turned out we had all had at least a few. In our dreams Lucy was never a ghost, not in any cliched way. She was no floating apparition, all see-through and blurry around the edges. In our dreams Lucy was essentially the same as she had been before she died, when she was working behind the counter of the dairy.

Ray told us that for several weeks in January of that first year he had a dream where Lucy walked into his science class. She stood next to Mr Mayer who was up the front, pointing with a ruler at a diagram of a volcano. 'I expected Mayer to ask her what she wanted but he just kept on talking. Everyone just carried on as normal. After a while I realised that I was the only one who could see her. She wasn't scary, but in the dream she just stared at me like she was kinda sad or something. Eventually I couldn't take it any more and woke up.'

We all had dreams that went something like that. Pete Marshall probably had the dreams most often that summer, which is understandable considering he was the one who found her body. He didn't say anything much at the time but spoke about it to Mark Murray. In Pete's dream he looked out of his bedroom window and saw that Lucy was standing over the road from his house under a flowering cabbage tree. She was wearing a red dress. She was staring up at his window, and when she noticed him looking out at her, she frowned. That was it.

They weren't nightmares, but they always woke us. They left us thoughtful and uneasy, unable to slip back into sleep. We lay in our beds, wrapped in the smell of rotting sea-lettuce. We listened to the wavesound and to the occasional cry of a wading bird disturbed on the estuary. We often lay for hours. It was no wonder that by the end of January we were all sunken eyed and edgy and feeling like ghosts ourselves.

People are usually willing to talk to us. That has been true right from the beginning. In fact, the people we interview often seem relieved to be able to talk. They want to unload what they know on to our shoulders. Almost inevitably they offer us up small details, tidbits that do not appear in any police interview or newspaper report. The details they remember for us maybe did not seem relevant at the time, or were thought to be too mundane to be chiselled in to official documentation. Maybe they sense our need for anything that will connect us to Lucy; that will enable us to see her more clearly through the mist that death (and now, the intervening years) has called down over her. In that sense, the information they dig out for us is like a gift for which we are always grateful.

We find that the unexpected question is the one that often draws out the truest response. That is why we approach people in their homes and while they are on the job. Sometimes they are on their smoko, sandwich in hand, or pausing to take stock before moving on to the next task. We have spoken to a housewife as she hung out wet sheets. We once interviewed the manager of a courier company on his way to work. He sat behind the wheel in his driveway, the engine of his car idling. One interview was even conducted on the sidelines of a club rugby match (New Brighton 21, Old Boys 12—a rare victory for the local club).

Of course, these days we almost never do interviews. They've all been done already, completed and filed down at the lock-up. Occasionally we will approach someone seeking clarification of some small point, but that can often be done over the phone. For years, though, we were the boys who appeared with pen and paper or—as we became older and more sophisticated—the young men with a chunky black tape-recorder lugged around on a shoulder strap. We have hours and hours of interviews on tape *Exhibits T1–T38).*

Mrs Asher only ever agreed to one interview, and that was only a couple of years ago, when she was seventy-one. We visited her at Calbourne Courts, a group of single-bedroom, concrete-block units arranged in a circle around a lawn, like covered wagons in an old western waiting to be attacked.

Even in old age, Mrs Asher still dressed in black. Possibly some of the clothes were the same ones she had worn when we were fifteen (Al Penny later referred to her as 'our own Miss Havisham'). Silver bracelets still hung on her wrists. But Mrs Asher's taut good looks were gone, replaced by a ballooning puffiness that had transformed her face and made her almost unrecognisable as Lucy's mother. Perhaps the bloating was a side-effect of her medication. Perhaps she had just chosen to let herself go after years of keeping up appearances.

Even though we were middle-aged men we felt the same awe in her presence as when we were fifteen and used to slip into her darkened dairy. We sat awkwardly in her cramped lounge and ate the soft Girl Guide biscuits she offered. We tried not to drop crumbs on the salmon-pink carpet. Mrs Asher sat in her big chair and spoke in what often seemed to be non sequiturs. She did not respond directly to any of the questions we asked her. She would share with us a story, which would gush from her mouth and then stop suddenly, as if a tap had been turned off. More often a rambling recollection was transformed midsentence into another about a completely separate incident from years before or years later.

It came as no surprise when Mrs Asher was officially diagnosed as having Alzheimer's. That was about eight months after we met with her. Al Penny visited her in the hospital unit where she is still living. He told the staff that he was her son. Nobody asked for

ID. Who but a relative would visit a woman like Mrs Asher? She was someone with neither a past nor a future.

Al found her sitting up in bed in the small, sparse room where she slept, wearing a shiny red house-coat with padded panels. For the whole visit Mrs Asher thought that he was her husband, even though by then Mr Asher had been dead fifteen years. Al tried to talk to her about Lucy, hoping that some small storm-tossed detail would be thrown up by her mind. But his questions only made her agitated. She kept talking over him, telling him that there was some loose iron on the roof that flapped in the wind at night and kept her awake. Her thin voice rose and fell like the probably imaginary wind that was bothering her. He would need to get up there and fix it, she said several times. Al finally promised that he would get on to it right away. Then she calmed right down and shortly after that Al made his excuses and left.

But on the day of our interview at Calbourne Courts Mrs Asher still had some of her mind left. The interview was so significant that all of us were there. Mrs Asher recognised Tug Gardiner straight away and asked how his father, her old neighbour, was. 'And is the dairy still there?'

Tug hesitated, unsure what to say, but in the end, settled for the truth. 'It closed down about eight or nine years ago. Too much competition from the supermarkets, I guess. The new people converted the shop back into bedrooms.'

Mrs Asher considered Tug through puffy eyelids. 'I always hated that shop anyway,' she said. There was a pause. 'Carrots are very hard to peel,' she added, and held up her hands to show us her swollen knuckles and twisted fingers. Whether her hands were proof or reason for the carrots' stubbornness we were not sure. We silently nibbled the edges of our soft biscuits while we thought about that.

Lucy, she told us a few minutes later, had always been a wilful child. 'Right from the very beginning she refused to bottle-feed. She knew exactly what she wanted and would howl until she got it.'

'We wish we'd known her better as a girl,' said Pete Marshall. We all nodded. It was true. Pete had come straight from work and was still wearing the white shirt from the Power Store he managed. His name badge was pinned to the pocket. Like most of us Pete had put on a bit of weight over the years. His shirt was tight over his gut where he had tucked it in to his belt and there were sweat stains under the arms.

There was another long pause. Calbourne Courts is over in the western suburbs and we listened in vain for the familiar scream of a seagull. The only noise was the hiss and rumble of the heavy trucks passing on the wet surface of the new motorway that had recently been built on the other side of the fence.

Mrs Asher seemed to find nothing unusual in re-counting episodes from her life to the half-dozen middle-aged men who had squeezed themselves into her small unit. But after an hour she tired and her stories began to be broken up by longer and longer gaps. When she was not speaking her head began to nod forward before snapping back up. Each time this happened she would look around the room wide-eyed as if seeing us for the first time. Sensing that we were missing our opportunity, Jim Turner asked if she knew anything she could tell us about the circumstances of Lucy's death. We all leaned forward.

Mrs Asher became suddenly guarded. She shuffled back into her big chair and fixed Jim with a look. Her eyes went small and sharp until they were almost lost beneath those puffed bags of flesh. 'She died,' she said emphatically and shook her head as though a fly had landed on her hair. 'My little girl died. That was the end of that.'

She told a few more half stories from the days when her daughters were young, before they went to school. It was a period that seemed lodged in her mind like a time of golden weather. But on Lucy's murder she would not be drawn. Finally she fell asleep. We stood quietly and filed out, shutting the door behind us.

We wondered if Mrs Asher would remember we had been there when she woke up. Perhaps the dented pillows and occasional biscuit crumb on the couch would be a source of confusion or intrigue to her. Would she even vaguely remember the group of inquisitive men who had appeared in her lounge, or would sleep, like an unusually high tide, wash her mind clean of memory's footsteps?

Perhaps Mrs Asher was right. Maybe there does come a time when that should be the end of that. Perhaps we should just let it go, stop digging when we have no map. It is not uncommon for one of us to promise himself that he's not going to carry on pursuing the investigation. All of us have had times in our lives when we've told ourselves we're not going to lose sleep thinking about it any more, or go through the files just one more time. We've persuaded ourselves that when we meet with the rest of the group for a beer or two, we're going to insist that we don't talk about anything to do with Lucy Asher. We've all had patches when we felt like that. Jase Harbidge went as far as suggesting that we form a support group, L.A.A.—Lucy Asher Anonymous. He was only half joking. Sometimes our abstinence lasts a few months. Mark Murray went a whole year and a half in the mid-nineties, before an article in the *Herald* about a case with some similarities to Lucy's brought him back into the fold.

Mostly our breaks are brought about by the feeling that there is no progress, that our lives are becalmed, although it is often wives or girlfriends who agitate enough to force a clean break. 'Creepy' is the adjective most often used by women. They resent the time we spend on the case, time they rightly feel is lost to them and to our families. But it is more than that: women sense that the Asher case is an area of our lives into which they can have no entry. It has been said many times over the years and in many different voices, and perhaps they are right; perhaps we should, 'get a life'.

But that is easier said than done. It would be fair to say that none of us has ever got over Lucy Asher. She was our first true love and, in some sense, our last. Of course we do not say that to each other in so many words, but we are aware that all of our lives are littered with troubled relationships with women. Break-ups and divorces seem to be par for the course, and at a rate that seems like more than statistics. More often than not, the place where we meet is the home of a single man whose kids visit at the weekend or whose new, often younger girlfriend resents our presence.

We can joke about it after a few beers. Our conversations are full of self-mocking and jokes at each other's expense. Occasionally our banter is close to the bone. But beneath the laughter, you can feel the undertow of tension and sadness.

The unspoken truth is that we are all still searching for something. Not just for Lucy's murderer, but for a moment in time when we had the unwavering belief that we served a higher purpose and a greater good. When you've had that, it's hard to let go. It's almost impossible to find any lasting satisfaction in the small details of a normal man's life.

You could even say that we are haunted by what happened back then. There are no rattling chains or shimmering visions. There are just our memories of a long hot summer, and the ghost of a broad-shouldered girl who swims in our blood and looks unlikely ever to leave.

Here's what happened to Pete Marshall last July. During his routine medical to get life insurance, they discovered the cancer that had started in his testicles and then hitched a ride in his blood up to his lungs. From there it had journeyed on to his brain. 'Riddled' was the word Pete used when he told us.

A few of us had gathered at Tug Gardiner's place to watch the Crusaders play in the final of last season's Super 14. We watched the rugby in the lounge over a bowl of Cheezels and bottles of beer. It was the same house we used to meet in when we were teenagers. Tug had been left the place when his father died. He could not bring himself to sleep in the room where his parents had conceived him, and where his dad had died of a massive stroke in 2003, so Tug still slept in the boxy room above the lounge where he slept as a kid.

Pete did the decent thing and waited to tell us until after the game. That was the joke that Jase Harbidge made in the seconds after Pete's words had drifted into the air like the black smoke from a bad neighbour's bonfire. We all laughed, including Pete, probably because we didn't know what else to do. But of course we were stunned mullets. We fumbled around for something to say that came close to matching our feelings. Pete let us off the hook by making light of the whole thing. He joked that it had him by the balls, but that he was going to beat it.

Of course you are, we agreed, grinning like hyenas faced with a lion. It's probably not as bad as the doctors think. They're always getting these things wrong. I heard of a bloke who ... and so on and so on until, when all the beers were gone and it was time to leave, we almost had ourselves convinced that Pete's condition was just a passing thing, like glandular fever or a bone broken in three places.

It was another of those gateway moments, like Lucy's funeral. At the time they are almost never recognised for what they are. People always assume that there will be another chance; that tomorrow will carry on pretty much the same as today. But, as the beer ad says, 'Yeah, right.' The bad jokes, and Pete's positive attitude, were our way of denying that Change had swept up behind us like a rogue wave and was now battering down upon us.

In the following days, and then weeks, we went on with our lives as normal. When thoughts of Pete tapped us roughly on the shoulder we shrugged them off. Of course, when we saw him we asked how he was feeling. 'Fine, better than ever.' And then, relieved to get that part over, we went back to business as usual. The first stage of grief is always denial.

THREE

It was common knowledge that on the night Lucy was murdered she had gone to the South Brighton Surf Club's Christmas party. The police questioned everyone at the party starting on the first day of the investigation. Their police interview notes are comprehensive and make interesting reading *(Exhibit T45–63).* Even so, we have our own interviews with everyone we've been able to establish was there that night. *(Exhibits T–A1–18).*

Brian Andrews, who in December 1980 was club president and holder of the national record for men's beach flags, remembered seeing Lucy dancing barefoot. He was twenty-four at the time, which seemed very old to us. The upstairs part of the surf club was just a wide open space with exposed rafters and a small kitchen with a Zip.

'I'd hung a disco ball up there, you know,' said Brian, twirling his finger slowly in the air. 'She was dancing with no shoes on. I remember thinking that she was going to be a real heartbreaker.'

Of course we'd demanded to know who Lucy was dancing with.

'With some of the other senior girls, by herself, with everyone. I don't know. It was a party, nearly everyone was dancing.' Brian shook his head sadly. 'Such a waste, eh.'

Pete Marshall's older brother Tony was also at the party, despite having only the most tenuous connection to the surf club. He had been a member when he was fourteen but had been kicked out for smoking dope on a carnival day, in the storage area under the club house. Tony admitted to us, but not the police, that he had smuggled several bottles of vodka into the Christmas party. Most of it had gone directly into the punch. He told us that as he slipped an empty bottle back into his bag, Lucy had suddenly been standing next to him, her face glistening and flushed from dancing. 'I thought she was gunna turn me in but she just laughed and helped herself to one of those big plastic cups of the stuff. "Cheers" that's all she said to me. Just "Cheers" which I thought was pretty cool. After that I didn't see her. There were a lot of people there.' Tony swept the long, dark hair from his face and looked us squarely in the eyes. 'Pity about what happened. Lucy was cool.'

Other people remembered Lucy from that night as well. Apparently she made an impression. Rachael White, who the next day was to faint so dramatically down on the beach, was sure Lucy was still at the party after midnight. 'She was dancing with lots of boys and not in a nice way, if you know what I mean.' (We didn't really, and frankly didn't trust Rachael's judgement.) 'I think she'd been drinking' was all the elaboration she would give.

When asked for specifics of who Lucy was dancing with, Rachael couldn't name a soul. But Tony Marshall immediately coughed up the name Anton Lester.

We spoke to Anton in the changing rooms after a cricket match. He had been in the same year as Lucy at school and that summer played for the second XI at the North Beach club. It was near the end of the season when we spoke to him. His team had just lost by fifty runs.

'Sure. I told the police. I danced with her for a while. She was a real tease—I thought I was in like Flynn. But then when we were out in the tower she got all frigid.' He undid the last strap from his shin-pad and threw it in the corner of the shower room before fishing his box out from the front of his trousers.

Out in the tower—that was something new. No one else had mentioned seeing Lucy leave the party. We bristled hearing him talk about her like that but wanted to know what had happened. Anton Lester misconstrued our interest. He grinned broadly and tapped the side of his nose with a finger stained red from bowling the new ball. (His mannerism seemed an obvious imitation of someone older, confirming our suspicion that he was a prat. 'For a while it was all good, then she said she didn't feel like it or some shit and she wanted to go back inside. I was pissed off but it didn't matter, a couple of hours later I nailed that White chick in the surf boat.'

And where had Lucy headed after that? Lester thought she'd gone back inside the surf club whose music and light must still have been spilling out on to the beach. But no one else we spoke to could remember seeing Lucy later in the evening. Not that this meant a lot. By then Tony's vodka had worked its magic. A swirling spell had been tossed over those people who were left at the party and to say that their memories were unreliable would be an understatement. The police concluded that Lucy left the party sometime between eleven and twelve and that she was alone. We have never found any evidence to the contrary.

The last reliable sighting of her was by Karen Wishart and Phil Foster. (*Transcript of Exhibit T63.*)

KAREN: Phil had driven his car to the party; he was just dropping me home.

PHIL: I was probably a bit pissed to drive but, you know, it wasn't like there were any bends.

[Note: This was a running joke on the Spit.]

KAREN: It must have been about two o'clock.

PHIL: Around about.

KAREN: Like we told the police, we were parked outside my parents' place.

PHIL: Just saying goodnight.

KAREN: Yeah. We saw Lucy in the street-light, just up the road.

PHIL: She must've come out of the dunes.

KAREN: She'd taken her shoes off.

PHIL: She was carrying them.

KAREN: She looked to me like she'd been crying.

PHIL: How could you tell that? It was dark.

KAREN: To me that's how it looked.

PHIL: Okay, fine.

KAREN: Then she turned and walked away. I thought she looked sad.

PHIL: Are we finished?

It was Al Penny who pointed out the obvious. 'Karen Wishart lives at number sixty-three, right, so if Lucy walked from the surf club and came out of the dunes near Karen's house then she had already gone past the dairy. And Karen said she turned and walked away. South. If she was heading straight home Lucy would've walked right past them.'

So where was Lucy going? The police reports we have contain separate interviews with Karen and Phil but the assumption seems to be that they saw Lucy as she was walking home. Without discounting other possibilities, the police have always worked on the theory that Lucy met her attacker somewhere between the surf club and her house, and then was somehow taken down to the channel. We now doubt that's the case.

Over the years we've often stood on the footpath at the spot where Lucy was last seen. We go there alone and in pairs, sometimes during the day but most often in the late evening after the street-lights have come on. Karen Wishart's family home was knocked down a while back and replaced by a row of three small townhouses. Apart from that the scene is pretty much the same as it would have been the night Lucy stood there barefoot. The track from the dunes still runs down between two sections. It's only a couple of metres wide and back in 1980 wasn't signposted. It's still hard to spot at either end, particularly with the way the sand is shifted around by the tides and the wind. Even today the track is seldom used by anyone except the locals, and surfers who know where to look. Lucy would have known it was there, of course, but it would have been tricky to find in the dark, especially at the beach end. That makes us think that she looked for it and was headed somewhere specific.

On warm evenings we sometimes stand there on that part of Rocking Horse Road and try to put ourselves in Lucy's shoes (sure, even though they were hanging from her hand). If we squint our eyes we can ignore the new townhouses and the late-model cars. It could easily be 1980 again, a summer night, five days before Christmas. What was Lucy thinking as she stood on this spot? Despite all our speculation, was she simply going for a walk to clear her head of Tony's spiked punch and then overshot her house? Unlikely: she had grown up on the Spit and knew the beach too well. Or was Lucy hoping that the additional exercise, about half a kilometre, would blow away the feel of Anton Lester's groping hands? But then why did she walk south on the footpath and not north past Karen and Phil?

We walk the routes she might have taken, starting at the surf club and then cutting in along the track. So she would have seen Karen and Phil's parked car about here. Did she know they were inside? Probably. She was only about five metres away and 'saying goodnight' can often get quite exuberant. It's possible she saw them before they saw her. And Karen thought Lucy had been crying. If that's right, why was Lucy crying that night? As we stand on Rocking Horse Road, unanswered questions flutter like summer insects around the street-light overhead.

So she turned and walked away along the foot-path. The street-lights are widely spaced. To Karen and Phil, or anyone watching her from a distance that night, Lucy would have vanished into the darkness and then reappeared in the spots of light. We don't know if she went all the way down to the reserve; we're unsure if she made it that far. It's possible she went into one of the houses. Was she stalked and then set upon by an opportunistic stranger as Al Penny has always argued? Or was Lucy going to meet the person would later kill her? That's the other possibility we toy with.

At the end of our nocturnal rambles we are in-evitably no closer to answering our own questions. We go home and slip into beds lying alone or some-times next to a long-suffering wife or girlfriend. The next day she may check our clothes for the scent of another woman and at the end of the month scan our credit-card statements for incriminating purchases.

That is part of the price we pay. We've learned not to take it personally.

By the end of January 1981 we had recorded three further sightings of Mr Asher at night in, or near, the dunes.

One day Mark Murray heard his mother on the phone in their kitchen. She was talking to Mrs Webb, Grant's mother. Mark's mum worked nights at the Wattie's factory where she performed the final inspection of the seals on the cans of vegetables. Mrs Murray had finished her shift at four in the morning and was driving home. Presumably she was tired. She would have been surprised, even shocked, to see Mr Asher caught in her headlights.

'There was no mistaking it was him,' she told Mrs Webb on the phone. 'Just crossing the road in the middle of the night like that. It gave me a real scare, I can tell you. Makes you wonder if he's still got all his marbles.'

She looked at Mark to see if he was listening. Mark was pretending to be reading the paper his father had left spread open at the sports pages on the kitchen table. Even so, his mother dropped her voice down to a whisper and Mark had to strain to hear.

'It's the strangest thing,' she continued, 'but I could've sworn he was carrying a baby.' And then she laughed loudly as if to dismiss the idea. 'I must've been staring at too many cans of beetroot.'

Despite his night-time wandering we knew that Mr Asher was still leaving the dairy every morning, six days a week. Tug reported that around nine, his battered ute reversed into the road and drove away, the toolbox rattling on the open deck. We had no idea where the job was that he was working on. The ute carried him beyond our borders, the channel and Thompson Park up at North Beach. They pretty much defined our territory.

As far as we knew, no one was missing a baby. 'What do you think it was that Mark's mum saw?' Pete Marshall wanted to know when we next met. 'What looks like a baby but isn't a baby?'

We all stood around in Tug's bedroom and shook our heads. It was a riddle that we didn't know how to unravel.

Tug had reported that there were lights on in the Ashers' garage most nights until two or three in the morning. Of course he had sneaked over there one night but the single window was boarded over, each board carefully overlapping the next so there were no gaps through which he could see inside. He could hear, though. He stood in the warm night and listened. Tug told us that it sounded like Mr Asher was doing some type of woodwork. There was sawing and hammering, broken by long gaps that the wavesound rushed to fill. If Mr Asher was building something, Tug had been left with no idea what it might be.

It wasn't just Lucy's father who was acting strangely. By the beginning of February Jase's father was officially on sick leave from the police. Jase didn't like to talk about it but we were all aware that Bill

Harbidge now seldom moved from his spot in front of the television. He cracked open the first beer of the day with breakfast and almost never left the house. With his mother run off it was left to Jase to cook the meals. He specialised in eggs (fried, poached, boiled or scrambled) and beans (tinned).

Jase's little sister, Charlotte, was eleven and kept asking him when their mother was coming back. She had learned not to ask her father. The results were too unpredictable. Sometimes the question would make him shout and swear. Sometimes—Jase told us, years later—he would start to cry, silent tears that wet his cheeks and made his big, loose-skinned face look as though it was melting down into his thick neck.

So it was Jase who washed Charlotte's school uniform and changed the sheets on her bed. He packed her lunches when school finally started back and showed her how to repair the punctured tyre on her three-speed. It was also Jase's job to buy his father's beer from the bottle store next to the supermarket. The manager was an old school friend of his father and would turn a blind eye. We would sometimes see Jase biking home with the crate balanced on the handlebars of his bike. By the end of March his father was simply tossing him the car keys, conveniently forgetting the fact that Jase hadn't yet sat his driver's licence.

One of the few things that Bill Harbidge did manage to do that summer, apart from changing the channel on the television, was contact an old mate of his who had left the police and gone to work in security. A couple of weeks later a brown envelope turned up in the letter box. It was Jase who found it and, curious, opened it. The photographs inside showed Jase's mother and the butcher doing everyday things. A couple were taken in the supermarket. Jase's mother is pushing a trolley in one shot while the butcher reaches up to take down a tin of something or other from a high shelf. In another she is sorting through a bin of apples. In another picture his mother appears to be weeding the garden in front of a small blue-and-white house, with a big tree by the gate. In yet another, the butcher and Jase's mother are sitting on a picnic rug on the grass, eating fish'n'chips. At first Jase could not tell why his mother looked so different. She almost seemed to him to be a different woman. It took him a while to realise that it was because in almost every photograph she was smiling.

January of' 81 rolled over into February. By the time school went back, during the second week of the month, it had not rained beyond a light drizzle. The days were not as hot as in the two preceding months but, even so, the classrooms' top windows regularly had to be cranked open to let in a breeze. The smell of the rotting sea-lettuce was still strong although the bloom seemed to have passed its peak by then. Teachers took to bringing cans of air-freshener to class and spraying it in clouds over our heads.

It worked for a while, but then the smell of the sea lettuce always crept back in.

We slumped at our desks in our grey shirts, unable to focus. The papers reported, in fewer and fewer column inches, that the police were following 'several lines of enquiry' into the identity of the Christmas Killer. We sensed the reporters' growing apathy. The number of detectives on the case had been scaled back. It was obvious they had made no real progress. Our own interviews and endless talk had circled around and around the same spots, leading us nowhere. The lack of forward movement made us torpid.

Looking out from our classrooms we could see a few scattered pine trees growing over in the dunes. The prevailing easterly gave the pines the low, sweptback look of the African trees we had seen on *Our World.* If we squinted, it was easy to imagine giraffes rocking slowly backwards and forwards against the blue horizon. Or the flick of a leopard's tail up in the lower branches.

For the first time we were beginning to think that Lucy's murder would never be solved, that our summer had been wasted. There was nothing new to be seen at the dairy and our supplies of money were exhausted. With our return to school Lucy's murder seemed to belong to a different era. Our teachers tried to instil in us a belief in the importance of the sixth form year but, as the tiny droplets of artificial lavender and rose rained down upon us, we were unable to muster any enthusiasm.

The only thing we were excited about in those days was the upcoming tour. It was almost certain now that the South Africans were coming. The Boks! For the first time in sixteen years the All Blacks' biggest rivals would play in New Zealand and we were over the moon.

For half the year, rugby was what our families talked about over dinner, what we watched together on the television, the spice in our lives. When the All Blacks toured we woke in the middle of the night to see the games. Still in our pyjamas, wrapped in blankets on the couch, with our fathers and brothers pushing in next to us, our voices lifting together, we urged Our Boys on from the dark side of the world.

Although the Boks weren't going to arrive in the country until July, the papers and the radio were full of talk about the tour. Most of it was political stuff and held no interest for us, although our fathers would watch the television coverage and mutter about 'stirrers' and 'commies'. All we knew was that the Springboks were the only team in the world that had beaten the All Blacks more than they had lost. There had been thirty-four test matches between the two countries and we had won only thirteen of them. The Boks had won the last two series—in 1970 and '76—three games to one. And now they were coming back. Now was our chance to even things up.

Although the weather was still hot we sought comfort in discussions of our winter religion. We talked about the selections at length. Who was going to make the All Blacks this season? Who was going to be in the Boks' touring squad? We speculated about the test venues. There would definitely be a test match at Lancaster Park, and we were confident that most of us would get to go. Over dinner our fathers told us stories about the big New Zealand versus South Africa clashes of the past. We hung on every word as they discussed heroes of the 1956 tour. Not many of us were used to our fathers talking for so long or with such animation.

All of us played rugby, with varying degrees of skill and success. Jim Turner was the best, by virtue of his size more than anything. At sixteen he was already six foot one and weighed eighty-five kilos. Jim had been selected to play at lock for provincial rep teams every year without fail since the age of ten. He was the only person ever to play for the school first XV while still in the fourth form.

Matt Templeton's father was head of the history department at our school and he also coached the first XV. He had played rugby at provincial level, where he had earned a reputation as an enforcer. He was a big man made bigger by his ginger beard and a huntaway voice. During the winter months, on Tuesdays and Thursdays after school, Mr Templeton could often be heard at full volume, yelling at his players as they trained: shuttles and sit-ups, passing and kicking, the intricacies of the rolling maul and the dragged-down scrum. Jim Turner's name often featured in these motivational lectures. Mr Templeton had been overheard on the sideline telling Mr Turner that his son lacked 'the killer instinct' that would elevate him to the elite levels of the game. He said someone needed to light a fire under Jim's arse.

It was Alan Penny, though, who knew the most rugby lore. He fed us the statistics about the Springboks: he could recite the scores from test matches going back twenty years. The names of the great players rolled off his tongue and he could recall even the most obscure rules. This was ironic, because in the course of an actual game Al was next to useless. He played for the school's Under Sixteen B team, but even then was often relegated to reserve. When he did get on the field he ran along the left wing, at the peripheries of the game, without purpose or intent. He was often at odds with the angle of the ball, or sometimes even the entire direction of play. Al gave the impression that he was someone out for a jog who had unexpectedly found himself in the middle of a rugby match. When the ball was inadvertently passed to him, Al's fingers were made of butter. Nevertheless, as our clippings about Lucy began to yellow and curl, Al gathered together all the information he could about the impending Springbok tour.

The second attack happened in broad daylight and on a weekday—to be accurate, at three forty-five on

Monday the twenty-seventh of February. Tracy Templeton, Matt's youngest sister and the last of our history teacher's seven children, was walking home from school with her best friend Jenny Jones. They were both eleven and had just moved up to form one at South Brighton Primary, which went up to form two. (Ninety percent of the kids went from there to New Brighton High in form three. Really it was only the Catholics who got shipped off to town for their high-school years.) In '81 during the first day of school Tracy and Jenny had found themselves sitting next to each other at the back of Mrs Shepherd's class. JJ and TT was what they started calling each other.

In those days there were no rows of chauffeuring mothers waiting outside the school gates come three o'clock; instead the streets around every school in the city were awash with kids heading home. They took up the whole footpath with their jostling, uniformed mêlée. Later, in the side streets, they broke off into trios or pairs. Sometimes the groups thinned out so much that they turned into a single kid walking home alone. Nobody thought anything of it.

The Bridge Street Reserve is an open area as big as a rugby field, with a kids' playground set back from the road: a slide and a seesaw and a five-seat metal horse that rocks backwards and forwards. There's also the community centre and the bowling club but they're on the far side. There are bushes and a stand of cabbage trees that drop long leaves the council workers have to pick up before they can mow. On the estuary side is a stand of pine trees that, if you walk through it, leads down to the water, or the mud if the tide is out.

Tracy Templeton told the police she and JJ weren't in the reserve, just walking along the road beside it, when she heard a noise and looked up to see a man with a dirty hat jump out at them. Before Tracy knew what was happening he had hold of her friend. Whether the guy was targeting Jenny Jones or he simply grabbed the nearer girl is impossible to say. Certainly Jenny was the smaller and by disposition shyer. To a predator lying in wait, Jenny Jones would have looked the easier of the two to bring down.

Tracy reported that the man at first grabbed Jenny by the arm but quickly changed his grip so that Jenny's back was against his chest and his left arm was across her throat. He wrapped his free arm around Jenny's waist and started to drag her backwards through the gap in the bushes. He must have been strong because he managed to lift her right off the ground, although he was later described as 'skinny, like a big boy'. Tracy said her friend was kicking like a non-swimmer who had got out of her depth.

The guy could have been any age from sixteen to seventy, Tracy admitted. She told the police that his hat had a wide brim and was pulled down low over his face. She got the impression that his hands and wrists were tanned, 'like a surfer or a Maori or something like that', which really didn't tell the police (or us) anything useful. He seemed to be talking into Jenny's ear. Although she wasn't sure, Tracy thought he might have been wearing a raincoat.

But you have to hand it to her. Most girls (or even boys) Tracy's age would have turned and run, hell for leather. Later they might have justified it as an attempt to get help, when actually the first impulse is always one of survival, to get yourself out of there. But being the youngest of seven kids makes you resilient, and Tracy Templeton wasn't intimidated by size. As Matt told us later his little sister had come out of their mother's womb ready to battle for a fair share of anything that was going.

As the guy dragged Jenny, one hand now burrowed under her skirt, Tracy followed them through the bushes. She didn't try to kick him or bite him or anything like that; she simply started screaming. Apparently it was a technique she had used before in her domestic battles. In our interview two weeks later we asked for a demonstration and she was happy to oblige. We were impressed by both Jenny's volume and pitch.

There are houses on both sides of the reserve and cars were passing on the road. The guy obviously thought Tracy's screaming would bring trouble for him, and sooner rather than later. In one movement he released his hold, turned and ran off towards the pine trees and the estuary. Jenny sat down hard on the ground and Tracy kept screaming until he was out of sight, just to be sure.

It took a little under half an hour for a police dog to be brought to the reserve. There was a small crowd there by that time and a number of rumours swirled around about what had actually happened. Grant Webb, on his way home from basketball practice, reported seeing the police dog sniffing around the base of the slide where the attacker may have waited for a while, smoking cigarettes and going over his plan. According to the official police report, the dog lost the scent at the edge of the water. The tide was high and the guy had been bright enough to wade in and use the estuary to cover his tracks. He may even have swum across to the other side.

On Rocking Horse Road people were already twitchy after Lucy's murder. One attack could be put down to bad luck, a lightning bolt out of a clear sky, the brakes that fail on the car you're driving home from the showroom. But two ... Everyone assumed that the guy who attacked Jenny was the same person who had murdered Lucy Asher. After that, Jenny and Lucy were regularly spoken of in the same sentence. How often did we hear our mothers say that it was only luck that stopped little Jenny ending up like poor Lucy Asher?

The certainty arose that a predator was, if not actually among us, then waiting close by. People eyed the long yellow grass of the dunes as though something crouched there. The darkness of the public toilets became a cave.

Some of us had sisters, and in later years we all dated girls from down the Spit. Without exception they could all recall the new rules and the lectures from parents after that attack on Jenny Jones. It was now dogma that they never talked to strangers. 'No, not even "hello."

'Keep your eyes down.'

'Keep walking.'

'Never *ever* get into a car!'

Such instructions were issued in every home, to girls as young as three.

Always move around in groups. Don't get caught out after dark. Don't go too far from an adult. Always tell someone where you're going and when you're due back and don't be late or we'll be worried sick. Avoid playing near the bushes or in the trees. Mum will be waiting for you at the school gates.

Overnight, the boundaries of childhood had shrunk.

But of course kids have questions. Why? was asked in a hundred different ways. What did the man want with Jenny Jones? What's wrong with the sweets? Are they poisoned like the apple in *Snow White?* What would the stranger do to me if he got me in his car?

The stories that parents told; the lies and half lies, the white lies and the grey lies and the black black truth. They told their kids everything from the generic 'hurt you', which was open to the most benign interpretation, right through to anatomically detailed descriptions of the act of rape.

For many girls these were the first conversations they'd ever had with their parents on the subject of sex. It was the birds and the bees. Except the way it was told down the Spit in late February of '81, the bird is an insatiable black crow and the bee will sting you again and again and again, and then leave you in a ditch for dead.

Through an informal network of neighbours, old team-mates and drinking buddies, the local men set up a community patrol. There were about thirty guys involved, including most of our fathers. There was a roster; four men each evening—there were enough volunteers that each name came up only once every couple of weeks. At the end of their working day, the men found themselves in groups of four, cruising the streets in a car, looking for anything suspicious. They often didn't have time to eat dinner so their wives packed food on plates covered with tinfoil. There was always a Thermos of coffee that was shared around. Normally there was beer as well. Everyone put in a small sum of money so that whoever supplied the car for the evening could have his petrol costs reimbursed. You can eat through a surprisingly large amount of petrol cruising slowly up and down the road.

We'd see them drive past as we went about our business. Their territory covered all of New Brighton, right from the bottom of the Spit all the way up past

Thompson Park and into North New Brighton. Sometimes the driver would pull the car over and someone's dad would lean out the window to talk to us. The patrols were always good-natured. The guys would joke around and the smell from the plates of food would waft out through the rolled-down windows. More often than not the guy doing the talking had beer on his breath. He'd ask us if we'd seen anyone unusual hanging around. Sometimes we had—a surfer we didn't recognise, or a guy with his dog, down in the dunes. The patrol always took what we had to say seriously, which we liked. They'd thank us and ask us to keep our eyes peeled and then drive off to check out what we'd reported.

They were looking for someone lurking in the shadows of the school grounds or a furtive peeper crouching outside a girl's bedroom window. They'd often pull over to talk to a stranger or a foreigner walking down the street. A couple of the guys would get out and have a chat. Officially, the plan was to call the police from the nearest house if the patrol spotted anything unusual. That was officially. But as we sat on our bikes with our feet on the footpath, or stood skateboard in hand and watched the car as it pulled away from us, we could hear the rattle of softball bats and golf clubs coming from the boot. None of us was naïve enough to think that the men were planning on fitting in a round of golf before they went home.

Our fathers and their friends cruised the streets until midnight and then returned home to get some sleep before work the next day. As we lay in our beds we would sometimes hear our fathers coming home; the creak from the front door and then footsteps, stumbly and slightly drunk, moving around the house. Our fathers would inevitably be drawn to the kitchen where they would muck around with bread and jam and whatever else they could find. Our mothers would often still be up and we would listen through the walls to their voices muttering together.

It was good to know that our dads were out there keeping everyone safe. We would roll over in our beds and try to get back to sleep.

The main organiser of the community patrol was, surprisingly, Bill Harbidge. Perhaps the attack on Jenny Jones had shocked him out of his downward spiral. Almost overnight Bill stopped drinking during the day and even his evening consumption seemed to have tailed off. He was still officially on sick leave but Jase would come home and find his father out in the garage pounding away on the stained punching bag that hung in the corner. Bill Harbidge had been an amateur boxer in his younger days. Jase would watch him shuffle around the bag with his guard up, jabbing away with his left and then letting loose with his right; what he called his 'cannonball'. The bag would swing a fair way when Bill Harbidge hit it with his right. The only thing that Jase reckoned let his dad down was his footwork. Bill Harbidge didn't dance like a butterfly any more. He didn't even dance like an old bear. He pretty much just stayed in the one spot jabbing away with his left and then unleashing that big right. Just a couple of minutes of jabbing and punching saw him breathing hard and his old sweatshirt from police training soaked with sweat.

When he wasn't hitting the bag or going for walks along the beach Bill Harbidge was on the phone to the local men organising who was going to provide the car that evening and who was going along for the ride. Bill drew up the roster for each week but on any given day guys were pulling out because of some emergency or other, or ringing Bill wanting to swap a shift with someone else.

Another one of our fathers who reacted strongly to the second attack was Mr Templeton, understandably, considering his youngest daughter was involved. Matt reported that after the attack his six sisters were under virtual house arrest. We'd all been taught history or social studies by Mr Templeton and knew that he was not someone you messed with. This was back in the days of corporal punishment and he was pretty handy with both ruler and strap, not hesitating to strap his pupils for talking in class or repeated lateness.

Matt's father had never been able to stand boys showing any interest in his daughters. Even before the attacks he'd actively discouraged those who came 'sniffing around'. He had once so badly beaten a boy he had found outside his eldest daughter's open window that the police had become involved. In the end no charges had been laid, but this incident had created an understandable caution among boys vying for the Templeton girls' affections.

It was a situation that Matt had been able to capitalise on. A short verbal message from a boy, delivered to one of his sisters verbatim earned Matt twenty cents. The reply cost the boy the same—C.O.D. Fifty cents was the going price for a written note. When boys tried to argue against the additional cost of putting pen to paper, Matt always told them the same thing: a note was more dangerous than a spoken message. 'With a note there's hard evidence. What if my father found it and forced me to say who it was from?'

No one argued after they heard that, not if they had any imagination. Matt Templeton had boys twice his size by the balls and they knew it. If you wanted to communicate with any of the Templeton girls the safest way was to go through Matt and then you paid the going rate. As we had learned in form three economics, it was basic supply and demand.

With five older sisters, all of whom were considered attractive and at least two of whom were widely rumoured to do much more than just kiss by the third date, Matt made a killing. He was by far the richest of our group. But he was generous with his money. When funds were needed for photocopying, or any of the other numerous expenses associated with our investigation, it was inevitably Matt who coughed up. A lot of the food we bought from the Ashers' dairy that summer was paid for by Matt's messenger business.

Matt also did a good line in alibis when one or other of the Templeton girls managed to sneak away to meet a boy. It was an additional service that he threw in at no extra charge. Matt could casually lie to his parents about Mary-Rose being at the movies or Annie staying over at a friend's house, without so much as blinking. After that his sisters were on their own. However, following the attack on Jenny Jones the Templeton girls found themselves locked down. Their father was moody and vigilant. He prowled the house like a hanging judge.

Of all the local girls only Carolyn Asher seemed to move about the neighbourhood at will. Tug would see her coming and going from the dairy at all hours. Sometimes she was picked up by a guy in a car. Often she wheeled her girl's bike with its low frame out the front gate and cycled off down the road, her long, pale legs often visible beneath her short skirts.

There were only rumours about where she went and what she did, but the stories we heard were becoming worse and reaching us more frequently. Even our mothers began to hear things. More than one of them warned us to stay well away from Carolyn Asher. Only a few months after her sister's funeral she was a girl with a reputation.

The only one of us who, at fifteen, claimed to have had sex was Grant Webb. He told a story that he repeated in slightly varying forms, about an exchange have had sex was Grant Webb. He told a story that he repeated in slightly varying forms, about an exchange student at a party his older brother had taken him to the winter before. Grant claimed that she found him irresistible and was all over him like a rash. We had heard from other sources though that the girl had drunk most of a bottle of tequila in the space of an hour. Grant was one of at least three guys who claimed to have had sex with her in an upstairs bedroom that night. The girl's name was Maria but pronounced strangely. Shortly after that party she stopped coming to school, abandoned her host family, and returned to the small French town where she'd grown up. What she made of her life after her visit here we do not know.

On a daily basis the closest we came to sex was Amy Trousedale. Amy was a solo mum who lived up past the intersection of Rocking Horse Road and Marine Parade. She was twenty-three and had twin boys called Jake and Zach. Back in the early eighties there was still some shame associated with being an unmarried mother. Girls who found themselves 'in trouble' were packed off to stay with aunts in other cities until the baby could be delivered and adopted out. Or more often, the girls were bundled along to special doctors where everything was sorted out, nice and tidy, in a couple of hours.

It was an open secret that Amy supplemented her meagre DPB with sex work. We had heard that a handjob cost thirty dollars. Word came to us through guys who had older brothers, who had friends, who claimed to have had been to Amy's house. For another twenty she would use her mouth as well and for a hundred bucks Amy would let you go all the way as long as you wore a rubber.

Our reason for wanting to interview her was simple. As Grant Webb said, 'If there's a sex pervert living in the area, then Amy's the one who's going to know who he is.' It was a logic we all understood.

Obviously we didn't want to simply turn up at her door. We had no idea of the hours that men visited her. We settled for talking to her at the playground where she took Jake and Zach most fine days. When Pete Marshall and Al Penny approached her, she was sitting on a bench watching her boys play on the seesaw. The truth was that Amy was not obviously sexy, even to fifteen-year-old boys. Amy was short and well on the way to being plump, with peroxide-blonde hair—what our mothers called a bombshell blonde. She always had bare feet in the summer. As she sat on the park bench her short legs did not allow her swinging feet to touch the ground and it was sometimes possible for Pete and Al to see that her soles were stained dark with the type of dirt that did not wash off from a single bath. She smoked constantly and, even at twenty-three, was beginning to get those thin lines at the corners of her mouth like collapsed under-runners. But despite Amy's lack of obvious allure she regularly featured in our fantasies. The knowledge that, with cash and a dollop of courage, we could find ourselves at the receiving end of Amy's favours was like an aphrodisiac poured into the local water supply.

Amy seemed amused when Pete and Al walked right up to her. Al had the tape recorder hidden in his school bag. He had put in a fresh tape and turned it on before they entered the park (the sound quality is poor but you can still make out what was said).

AL: We'd like to talk to you.

AMY: How old are yous?

AL: Fifteen.

AMY: Come back when you're sixteen.

PETE: About Lucy Asher.

AMY: Who?

PETE: The girl who was killed.

AMY: Hang on.

It is noted on the transcript that at that point Amy went over to break up a fight between her boys and another kid. You can just hear muffled shouts and some distant crying on the tape. Jake and Zach were four, and big for their age. They dominated any playground they were at, like miniature mob enforcers. Right from when they could first walk they had pushed and gouged and bashed kids twice their age. They threw bark and sand in the faces of other kids and, if challenged, in the faces of the other kids' mothers. They bit like pit-bulls. Girls and boys alike lived in fear of the Trousedale twins—they were equal opportunity bullies. And when they weren't fighting other kids, they were bashing each other. These days most of us have got kids of our own and, looking back, we now realise how those boys must have made Amy's life hell.

AMY: So what did you guys want?

AL: We thought you might have some information.

AMY: I didn't know her.

AL: [Unintelligible] younger.

AMY: She wasn't a friend of mine or anything.

PETE: She was raped.

AMY: So?

PETE: We thought you might know something.

According to Pete she just stood up and walked away. He said later that he knew they had offended her but he wasn't sure how. On the tape you can hear her shouting something at her boys in the background. The words '...you'll brain-damage him' rise clearly out of the static. Pete and Al left the park as the twins began rolling pinecones down the slide with a sound like an approaching stampede.

When they got to the road, Al reached into his pack and turned off the tape recorder. He told us he looked back and saw Amy standing by the swings staring in their direction. 'She looked tired and sad. I kinda felt sorry for her.'

However, we were not going to be put off that easily. We reasoned that Amy wasn't going to simply hand over details of her clients. As with lawyers there was probably some agreement about confidentiality, 'or like doctors have with the Hypocrite's Oath,' was how Mark Murray put it (the 'Hypocrite's Oath' is still something we like to bring up every now and then when Mark gets a bit cocky).

We took to watching Amy's house. It was just a small Summerhill stone place, which she rented. There was a vacant section right next door so we loosened boards and enlarged knotholes in the fence and took shifts sitting in the long dry grass after school. Her clients were not as regular as we had expected. In the first three days there was only one guy who might have been visiting for sex. He arrived at 9.30 in the evening, close to the time when we were about to give up for the day. He parked his car up the road and entered Amy's place on foot, walking so quietly that we almost missed him. He knocked gently and slipped inside. The blinds were already pulled and we couldn't see a thing.

He left an hour later and although we got a better look at his face none of us recognised him. He looked surprisingly normal. Just in case it came in useful, we recorded the details of his car: make, model and number plate. But we never saw him again. After he had left, Amy came out in her dressing gown. Her hair was wet as though she'd been in the shower. She put her rubbish bag down on the footpath and without looking around went back inside.

We were beginning to learn that investigative work is mostly boring. It's all about accumulating small details over long periods of time. The facts gather like dust on a windowsill until there are enough to see. Every day after school for two weeks we sat in the flattened grass, doing shifts of two hours each. Sometimes we were alone; sometimes one or more of the others came down because they had nothing better to do. We read comic books or played backgammon. Pete had been sent a backgammon board for Christmas by his brother Tony, who was in the navy by then. Tony had picked it up in Sydney when his ship had visited there on some Australia – New Zealand joint training manoeuvres.

Eventually we came to see a pattern in Amy's days. She saw clients from Monday to Friday. Amy started work at around eight o'clock in the evening. Presumably Jake and Zach went to bed early, exhausted by a hard day terrorising the neighbourhood. They probably never met the men who visited their mother. There were one or maybe two guys most evenings. Sometimes there would be none and Amy's bedroom light would be switched off early.

By the end of the second week we were bored and ready to give up. The only conclusive thing we had was a list of car licence plates. The guys who visited her were mostly middle-aged and completely normal-looking. There were no obvious murderers, no screams in the night. As Mark Murray asked, 'What the hell does a sex pervert look like anyway?' We began to feel foolish for even thinking that we would discover anything by watching Amy.

It was a Friday and, we had all agreed, the last evening before we'd give up watching her for good. Tug Gardiner and Jase Harbidge were watching the house. Tug thought at first that Bill Harbidge must have been there on police business. But Jase's dad was not in uniform and there was no sign of a police car. In fact, he seemed to have arrived on foot, emerging out of the dunes.

'His hair was combed,' Tug said, 'and you could smell the Old Spice from where we were.'

Jase went quiet, Tug added, and left on his bike soon after his father had gone inside. There was no real betrayal involved. It didn't look like Jase's mum was coming back. Nonetheless we knew that it was a humiliation for Jase. Actually, it disturbed us all. If Jase's father, a policeman, could feel that inner tension that moved him to knock quietly on Amy Trousedale's door, then couldn't those same feelings be stirring in our own fathers? Who was to say that our dads didn't, from time to time, pop out on some errand and then find themselves parking the family car down the road and walking back to Amy's house?

That was the last time we ever watched Amy. Without discussing it, we knew that it was better not to know for sure. We even started avoiding passing by her house in the evenings in case we should see something we didn't want to. We never spoke of seeing Bill Harbidge there, and not just because it would embarrass Jase. There was more than our friend's feelings at stake. We had started to see that there were shadowy places all around us that were better left undisturbed.

FOUR

March brought the first real rains of the year. For four days, Wednesday to Saturday of the first week of that month, the rain fell almost continuously. It varied between sheets of windblown mist and heavy drops that pockmarked the sand. By the end of that week the dunes had changed from summer's tired yellow. They now wore a shade of green we could barely remember from last spring. The tussocks stood tall and the ice plant was no longer soft and limp but pointed plump fingers at the sky. Moisture clung to everything so that as we moved around the dunes our school socks got soaked.

March also brought the sea fogs rolling in off the Pacific. Sometimes the fog covered the whole coast, sometimes just New Brighton and occasionally only the Spit. It could linger for a few hours in the morning, or for a whole day. Once or twice that year it draped itself over the coast for several days on end so that we lived our lives in a twilight world.

The goal posts had only been up for few days when someone attacked the local rugby club under cover of the fog. By then even we were aware that there were some people who felt strongly that the Springboks should not be touring at all. We had no time for this point of view. As Pete Marshall's father said, 'Sport is sport and politics is politics.' But apparently some people didn't agree. On the first Monday in

March we went down to the rugby grounds to see the damage for ourselves. Someone had written the word APARTHEID in bright red paint across the front of the clubrooms. The down stroke of the T cut right through the middle of the door. Even worse though was what they had done to the grounds. They must have used a pretty strong weedkiller. The grass from one twenty-two-metre mark right up to the halfway line was dead in patches. Standing close it was hard to see what the oversized letters spelt but when we stood up on the top of the natural embankment we could read two words. STOP TOUR.

Nearly everyone down the Spit was outraged. It felt like a random act of terrorism. What type of people came in the night and defiled such an important part of the community? But more and more we were seeing signs of anti-tour behaviour. Occasionally on the bus we would see someone wearing a red, white and black Halt All Racist Tours badge. We looked at the wearers curiously but there was no discernable type that we could see. There were badges on both men and women, on people who were well off, and on university lefty types. They were even being worn by some retired people who we believed should have known better. We wondered which one of them had been responsible for vandalising the rugby field but found it hard to visualise people so normal-looking out on the grass in the night spraying weedkiller. We believed that we would know a fanatic when we saw one.

Shortly after that posters started going up in New Brighton. At first they were only put up at the shopping centre and then they crept south on the lampposts.

STOP THE TOUR! RALLY AND MARCH THOMPSON PARK SOUTH BRIGHTON 8 June 6.30pm

Because of the attack on the rugby grounds we felt that these posters belonged to an unseen enemy. We pulled them down and stuffed them into rubbish bins whenever we could. We even ripped them up into small pieces so that they could not be taken out of the bins and recycled. Within a few days fresh signs would go up and we tore those down too. But it seemed that whoever was putting up the posters had an endless supply.

It was Al's idea to talk to Sarah Fogarty about Lucy's murder. 'If anyone's going to know something, it's her.' It was an obvious idea and we wondered why we hadn't thought of it earlier. All the boys at South Brighton High School were habitually wary of Sarah. She had an aura of disdain for all things masculine and had been known to hit boys who annoyed her, hard enough to deaden arms. We all agreed that she had been an unlikely best friend for Lucy Asher.

Matt was our emissary to Sarah solely because of his six sisters: he was well versed in the high rituals of young women. Matt found Sarah Fogarty at the school tennis courts. Unusually for a girl in those days she was alone. She was busy hitting a ball against the concrete practice wall. When Sarah first came to our school in the fourth form, after her family had moved up from Geraldine, she had been a champion tennis player. She had regularly beaten girls three years older. Gradually, however—and for reasons known only to herself—Sarah had given the competitive side of the sport away and now played only for fun.

When Matt approached her, Sarah was hitting the ball forehand with all the ferocity of her previous match-winning form. He told us later that the ball slammed into the wall at almost the same spot every time. He waited.

'Well?' she said, when it was at last clear that Matt was not going away. She spoke without looking over at him.

'I wanted to talk to you about Lucy.'

'No fucking shit.' Another reason boys were wary of her was Sarah's disconcerting ability to out-swear even the toughest boys. 'Can't you see I'm busy here?'

'We were wondering if you knew who killed her?'

As investigative work goes it was pretty crude stuff, but at least the question made Sarah stop hitting the tennis ball. It bounced back off the wall and rolled across the ground past Matt's feet, coming to rest at the foot of the umpire's chair in a puddle left over from the recent rain. Sarah looked at Matt for the first time. He told us that she had the sunken bruised eyes of Ali losing to Holmes. According to Matt Templeton, Sarah looked as though she had hadn't slept for a year.

'If I knew who fucking killed her I'd tell the police.'

Matt didn't comment. His place at the bottom of an entirely feminine pecking order had taught him when to stay silent. Sarah walked over to retrieve her ball. She had to pass close to where Matt was standing and he tensed up, waiting for her to plant her knuckles in his arm. But Sarah simply picked up the wet ball and went back to hitting it against the wall.

Thump. Thump. Thump. Interspersed with the twanging of the strings.

Matt waited for a long time but Sarah didn't say anything else. It was clear to him that she could go on hitting the ball all day.

He was outside the tall wire fence and walking away when Sarah called out to him. 'Hey, shit-head!' He turned back and saw that she was standing by the fence, her racket hanging loose in one hand. Even from a distance he could see Sarah's cavernous eyes and they made him shiver.

'She was seeing some guy but she wouldn't tell me, who.' And then she turned away, leaving Matt feeling as shaken as he would have if Sarah had hit him after all.

The news that Lucy Asher had been seeing someone, and all that implied, caused a wave of consternation to wash through Jim Turner's garage. It tarnished those memories of Lucy we had assembled and now jealously guarded. Other images came, unbidden and unwelcome. Grant Webb openly asked about the possibility of Lucy having 'done it' but was hissed down. He retreated into sullen silence. The idea was an insult to the Lucy we had breathed life into during the hot pungent summer.

At fifteen, we saw sex everywhere. It hovered near Amy Trousedale, of course, but also near every halfway attractive girl passing on the street. We watched all the girls and women in togs down on the beach, and gazed at every scantily-clad model on a billboard, magazine cover or TV ad. Every off-colour joke we heard our fathers make in passing, every flick and pout, every giggle and bare-legged step seemed designed to turn us on. The whole world was like one big subliminal message. But Lucy Asher was different. Lucy was exempt from our hormonal obsessions. We could not believe that Lucy was part of the guilty world of our fantasies. Lucy's name did not belong in the same sentence with that of Amy or any of those other women. They were like different species. They swam in the same ocean, but at different depths. By consensus, we decided that if Lucy had a boyfriend then it must have been someone who took her to the movies a couple of times, maybe held her hand—certainly nothing more.

We were inclined to want to push this new information to the back of our minds but Pete Marshall said, 'It's our first real clue. We've got to follow it up.

We owe it to Lucy.' It was after school on the day Matt had spoken to Sarah Fogarty. We were back in the garage, not having met there as a group for several weeks. By then Mark Murray had found an old picture-frame in a storage box and brought it along to the garage. Al Penny, who had become the unofficial custodian of all the news reports and interview notes, had transferred the photo of Lucy printed in *The Press* into the frame. We covered the work bench at the back of the garage with a tasselled table cloth that hung down to the concrete floor. The frame was painted gold and still had its glass and Lucy smiled out at us. The silver trophy sat next to the photo. Above the bench, pinned to the unlined walls of the garage, were the carefully trimmed articles from the newspapers.

Pete Marshall's words made us feel guilty and our eyes dropped. 'We owe it to Lucy,' he said again. He was right. So, together, we compiled a list of possible suspects. Boys Lucy could have been seeing who, we assumed, could have gone on to be her killer. Unlike the police, we were not constrained by lack of evidence or even the need for objectivity. The slimmest connection to Lucy, the whisper of a rumour, a hunch or old prejudice, saw boys named. They were secretly photographed and their faces hung in the Turners' garage on what became known as 'the boyfriend wall'.

All the photographs were taken by Al Penny with the second-hand camera he got for his birthday that year, a Pentax ME Super. Al got very good at taking pictures to do with the case. The camera didn't have a great zoom on the lens but he had an instinct for the impending moment when all the variables would slip into place. He had a shy boy's knowledge of how to get in close without being seen.

By the end of March we had nine photographs pinned to the wall. All the boys were from New Brighton, all were roughly Lucy's age and, with the exception of one, all had recently attended our school. Luckily, all of them still lived at home so we were able to spy on them. They were photographed through bus windows or as they got out of cars. Al caught them on street corners or through the windows of their homes as they ate dinner with their families. Several were photographed on the beach, surfing or swimming; one as he dozed in the sleep-out behind his parents' house.

Looking back, it is clear that we displayed little imagination in our choice of suspects. Without exception they were good-looking young men. More often than not they were respected rugby or cricket players. Our reasoning was that if Lucy had been going out with anyone, why wouldn't it have been with one of these guys? Only Matt Templeton argued that our choices were flawed. Girls—all girls—he argued, went for the outsider, the maverick, the Han Solo type. To back up his claim he brought along a poster belonging to one of his older sisters, Mary-Rose. The poster showed James Dean walking along a footpath in the rain. He was looking cool and tough, yet a bit dishevelled like he'd been awake all night. He also looked slightly lonely. 'That's the type of thing girls really go for,' Matt said. We were interested. Because of his sisters he was by far the most qualified among us. Here was information, if not straight from the horse's mouth, then certainly from the donkey who lived in the next-door paddock.

On the strength of Matt's recommendation we included Steve Weldon on our list. Steve had been in Lucy's year at school but had left at the beginning of the sixth form in a torrent of controversy and speculation. The school never came out and said why Steve was 'asked to leave' and there were a lot of myths that grew up around the episode. Whether he really had used his locker key to scratch a jagged FUCK into the side of the headmaster's orange Datsun is uncertain. It may have been Steve who released the twenty doomed frogs from the biology room into the space above the hung ceilings. (Their gentle croaks could be heard coming from above our heads for weeks, in classrooms as far away as the English department.) Whether it was for one of these acts of minor rebellion, or for something else entirely, all anybody knew for sure was that in the July of his University Entrance year, Steve Weldon's arse was grass.

One fairly typical photograph we have of Steve shows him wearing tight black jeans and a black AC/DC T-shirt with a skull on the front. As far as fashion statements went, we all agreed it was pretty cool. In the photo he is standing outside his mother's house, where he lived at the time of the murder, waiting for the mailman to arrive *(Photo Exhibit P36 SW).* He's been photographed slightly in profile. His mouth is partly open as though he is tasting the salt air. If you look carefully you can see his chipped front tooth. Steve had never attended another school after leaving ours and, as far as we knew, never got a job. How he spent his time was a subject of frequent speculation.

No one could collaborate a definite sighting of Steve Weldon and Lucy together but we agreed that didn't exclude them from having been in a secret relationship. Roy Moynahan went so far as to argue that no one ever having seen Lucy and Steve together was in itself suspicious, and possibly proof that they *were* seeing each other. But that was a bit philosophical for most of us. That Steve was the coolest boy down the Spit was enough to get him on our list.

We still kept track of the other boys on the boyfriend wall but as the weeks went by we came to focus on Steve Weldon more and more. Not because his behaviour was that of a murderer—he was no more suspicious in his day to day behaviour than anyone else—but because we quickly became fascinated by him. Steve turned out to be living a life that was almost totally different from our own.

Towards the end of March and the beginning of April we took close to sixty photographs of Steve Weldon. Most of them are mundane. He is shown standing out the back of his house, under the eaves, smoking a cigarette (he had a pack-a-day habit); eating an ice cream; sitting on the seesaw in the deserted playground; peeing against a lupin in the dunes during one of his rambling walks. We came to realise that his days were largely empty spaces waiting to be filled. Life without school was a series of linked meanderings and minor chores.

There were only two things that seemed to animate Steve. The first was his motorbike. He rode an old Triumph, which he maintained himself. The Weldons' garage door was almost always open, the floor littered with the greasy entrails of Steve's bike. We came to suspect that he took his bike apart even when it was running smoothly, just to fill his long, unfocused days. Most evenings when the bike wasn't in pieces he would take it out for a run. He would roar out of the gate and the sound would recede until it mixed with the sound of the waves. We were never around late enough to see him return.

Surprisingly, the other thing Steve enjoyed doing was cooking. His father had died of a heart attack at the age of forty-two (around the age we are now). His mother was a pug-faced woman who seemed to have been constructed out of heavy lumps of white dough. She worked long hours as a cleaner but when she came home each night Steve would have a meal on the table. And not just the meat and three veg that was the meal-du-jour every-day down the Spit. Steve Weldon regularly served his mother up fettuccine, lasagne, crêpes Suzette and chicken breast stuffed with apricot. He made her exotic dishes in the days when most men couldn't boil an egg, and when even our own mothers thought chow mein was a town in China.

'Sure, I knew you guys were watching me but I didn't care.' Our interview with Steve was held in April 1989, after he returned from a stint working in London. We asked him where he used to go on his bike in the evenings. 'I liked to get out on the open road. Sometimes I'd drive south to Ashburton or go inland to Hanmer. Once, I remember, I drove all the way to Nelson and then just turned around in front of the cathedral and came back in the dark. It was something to do.'

We were watching the Weldon house on the evening Carolyn Asher first rode up on her bicycle. She laid the bike against the scrappy macrocarpa hedge and walked up the drive as though she'd visited there every day of her life. 'I was in the garage and she just walked right up to me and asked to go for a ride. Yeah, I knew who she was. I knew what had happened to her sister.'

We wondered if he knew more than that, if he had heard the stories about Carolyn. But we were willing to give Steve the benefit of the doubt. We imagined her clinging to him, her long, bony body pressing into his back, looking ahead over his shoulder, leaning into the corners with the night air buffeting her face. Where did they go? What did they do when they got there? Even years later, Steve Weldon wouldn't tell us. All he would say was that they talked a lot and that it was private.

Carolyn Asher started to appear at the Weldons' house almost daily, always when Mrs Weldon was at her cleaning job and Carolyn herself should have been at school. She had been missing a lot of school that year, something that neither the system nor her family appeared to be doing anything about (and okay, we were missing some ourselves). Steve told us that they were 'friends, during a difficult phase in both our lives'.

One of the most interesting things Steve would tell us was that he had once caught Carolyn in his room going through his stuff. He asked her what she was looking for, but she wouldn't say. Of course, by the time we interviewed Steve we knew. Even when she first turned up at his house we were beginning to get an idea. Carolyn was looking for clues. She was searching for that letter or the stolen ring or a lock of snatched hair. Anything that would link Steve to her dead sister.

It was clear that Carolyn Asher had her own list that she was working her way down. Her list and ours overlapped in places. We envied her direct access, the laissez-faire way she strolled into guys' lives and took what information she wanted. In contrast, we were forced to hover on the peripheries with our binoculars and camera, speculating and drawing inferences, snapping blurry photographs and sorting through rubbish bins by the light of torches.

But Carolyn Asher's investigation was taking its toll on her. By the beginning of April she was looking permanently tired, the skin on her forehead had become almost transparent and the thin blue veins beneath were clearly visible. We wondered if she was eating. The hours she was keeping seemed to suggest she wasn't sleeping that much. She had begun to move with a leaden grace to her own slow music. By the time she had worked her way down her list to Steve Weldon, Carolyn no longer had the intensity we had seen at Lucy's funeral. She had become dreamy and detached.

'Caro was kinda screwed up,' Steve commented, 'but I really fell for her, you know.' That was the end of the interview 'Good luck. I hope you find what you're looking for.'

By the beginning of May Carolyn no longer came to visit Steve. We understood her pattern by then. Just like us, Carolyn Asher had crossed Steve Weldon off her list of suspects. Steve tried to see her again but she made it clear it was over.

By May we had almost a dozen recorded sightings of Mr Asher at night down on the beach or in the dunes. The hammering and sawing went on night after night in his garage so apparently he too wasn't bothering with sleep any more. Sometimes he would appear in car headlights as he walked down the middle of the road, like an animal seen on night safari, face turned towards the approaching car, eyes bright, before moving away into the darkness. If he was heading towards the beach he was almost always carrying a large bundle. We still had no idea where the baby fitted in to the whole jigsaw.

Mrs Asher was still working in the dairy. By then it was habitual for people to avoid the place and it was a matter of public speculation how long the Ashers would be able to keep it open. Mrs Asher's thinness had moved beyond surprising. She now shocked everyone who saw her, although that wasn't many people in those days because of the lack of customers and because as far as anyone knew she never ventured beyond the front door. We were now only sporadic customers ourselves: there were whole weeks when we couldn't bring ourselves to go inside. Mrs Asher now seemed to haunt the place. Occasionally Tug would see her pass, floating like an apparition, in front of the dark windows. We wondered if it were possible for a person to grow so thin that they simply disappeared, blown away perhaps on the easterly.

Mr Asher no longer bothered with maintenance. Tiles began to slip from the roof, catching in the guttering before eventually falling into the long weeds at the side of the house. The back lawn was never mown. The windows were dim with blown sea salt and sand, so they let in even less light. The paint on the outside walls blistered and popped in the corrosive air.

All things considered, the Ashers were not coping well.

We had also stopped going to Tug's room much. Apart from the slow fall into disrepair there was nothing new to see at the Ashers', and what we could see was depressing. However, we sometimes still gathered in the Turners' garage after school and in the evenings to play pool and muck around with the weights. We were there one Sunday early in May when Pete Marshall came bursting in. He had made another discovery on the beach. This time he *was* out for a training run. Pete played at centre for the third XV and had been running on the beach two or three times a week as well as training after school on a Wednesday.

Pete carried in what he had found, wrapped in a towel. We all stopped what we were doing and crowded around to see. It was a raft or, rather, a scale model of a raft made of driftwood and lashed together. There was a mast and intricate rigging made out of string and a canvas sail that at some point had been ripped almost free. The thing that we all noticed was that the raft was very well made. It hadn't been thrown together but rather crafted by someone who had chosen the wood carefully and then assembled it with care. The driftwood was smooth and it had been evened off with a saw at each end so that the raft was rectangular. The pieces were lashed together with intricate knots. The mast was straight and the rigging quite complex. There was even a deep centreplate that poked down through a slot in the middle: it would make the raft more stable in the water and help it travel in a straight line.

Sitting on the raft was a doll. It had been tied to the mast with wire that was wrapped around its body, under the arms. It was one of those dolls that guys with sisters knew well; the type with a plastic head and a soft, floppy body. Its eyes closed when you laid it back and opened when it sat up. There were clothes you could get to dress them but this doll had nothing on. It was just the blue cloth body and the hard head with the long blonde hair matted together.

'I saw it being rolled over in the surf,' said Pete.

This explained Mrs Murray's sighting of Mr Asher with a baby. Recalling the heap of dolls Roy Moynahan had seen in Lucy's bedroom, we wondered how many of these her father had launched out into the waves. We speculated that Mr Asher waited for a calm night with an offshore breeze so that the sail would carry his rafts beyond the waves. The current in the channel when the water was flowing out of the estuary would help push them into the ocean. Even so we knew enough to doubt that any of them had made it far. Most of them had probably only travelled out a few kilometres before being pushed back to shore by the current or when the wind inevitably changed back to the east. They would mostly have ended up like this one, swamped on the beach and pounded by the surf, or broken against the rocks somewhere down south.

Even so, over the years it has always been tempting to imagine one of Mr Asher's rafts beating the odds. We like to think of one of Lucy's dolls, her favourite perhaps from a happy time in her childhood, surviving all the perils: the big waves; the rockbound currents; the bow waves of passing tankers. It is pleasing to imagine one of them riding the ocean for weeks, months, even years, on the small but sturdy vessel that Mr Asher had lovingly made in his garage.

'But what's the point?' asked Grant Webb on the day Pete found the raft. He turned it over in his hands and inspected the underside. 'Why does he make these things?'

Nobody bothered trying to explain it to him. If you didn't get it when you saw it, you probably never would.

We weren't treating Mr Asher as a suspect any more so it was only luck that we discovered where he went every day. Mrs Murray took Mark shopping one Saturday morning. She had asked her son along to help carry the bags, which was just a red herring. Really it was another of those attempts by our mothers to spend time with us. There was a phase when they all asked us to help them with jobs around the house, or to go with them in the car somewhere. Anything so they'd be alone with us. 'How are things going?' they would ask, when the time seemed right.

They were desperate for some of the old intimacy. They must have remembered clearly the days when they had been our whole world and we had talked to them about every scratch and every shiny stone. Even at the age of eleven most of us were still being read to and giving our mums a goodnight kiss. Just a few years later our mothers were hanging out for a bad knock-knock joke. Of course we had nothing to say to them in those days. We were as closed as prodded shellfish.

The supermarket in New Brighton where Mark's mother took him was next door to the Empire Hotel. The Empire was, and still is, one of those massive, boxy buildings on two levels. It had a pub downstairs with a restaurant, and cheap rooms upstairs. It was at the public bar of the Empire that our fathers drank after work on a Friday. And it was from there that they often returned home for a late dinner, smelling of beer and slapping our irritated mothers on the backside, right in front of us.

As he was loading his mother's shoping into the boot of their car Mark caught sight of Mr Asher's ute. It was parked over in the car park of the Empire, but near the back next to the fence where other cars would normally stop you seeing it from the road. But from the supermarket car park Mark had a clear view: it was quite early in the morning (Mark's mum liked to beat the crowds) and Mr Asher's was one of the only vehicles. Seeing the ute there got him to thinking.

On Monday morning Mark and Jase Harbidge set off for school as usual but soon veered off and pedalled north on their bikes the half-hour it took them to get to the Empire. Jase reported that they waited, and sure enough Mr Asher pulled into the car park at nine thirty. He parked his ute in exactly the same space where Mark had seen it on the Saturday. They watched as Mr Asher sat behind the wheel staring straight ahead at nothing in particular. He just sat in the car park waiting until the Empire's manager unlocked the door. Then he got out and walked straight in.

Mark and Jase could see the bar through one of the big sash windows. They crouched down and watched as Mr Asher sat at a table in the far corner. He was drinking something from the top shelf, which he went up to the bar to get. There was no one else in the place until eleven o'clock and then only a couple of sad old alkies. Mark and Jase were still there at lunchtime when a group of office workers came in for lunch but they stayed in the other room, which had a sign over the door reading *Restaurant.*

Mark and Jase camped out over the road under the awning of a rock shop. There were quartz crystals, two for three dollars, advertised in the window. According to Mark they kept a close eye on the Empire in case Mr Asher decided to leave. Occasionally one of them would wander across and look in the window. 'But we needn't have bothered. Apart from getting refills, Mr Asher didn't move from his table.' From what they said he didn't even bother looking around the room.

By early afternoon they were bored and went into the rock shop, where they sifted through the boxes of loose crystals and polished stones. They were the only people in the shop. Mark asked the lady behind the counter to unlock a display case and she took out a fossilised shark's tooth the size of his hand. When it became clear that they weren't going to buy anything the woman got snippy and told them to leave. They went back to sitting on the footpath, staring across at the Empire.

Mr Asher finally left at four thirty. Beyond a slight fluidity to his walk, he didn't appear to be drunk. 'But he must have been totally sloshed,' Jase commented (and because of his dad, Jase would have known). Mark and Jase watched Mr Asher get into his ute and drive away in the direction of the Spit.

To most of the men living down New Brighton the organisers of the anti-tour march were nothing more than a group of stirrers. Our fathers and their friends had a deep-seated distrust of any sort of organised protest. On principle they didn't like speeches and rallies. They were suspicious of boat rockers. Tug Gardiner's dad said over a plate of mashed potato and lamb chop that they were 'Commie dyke stirrers, to boot. What good will a bunch of lefties marching up and down Marine Parade do? They aren't going to change what's going on in South Africa one little bit. They're just going to piss people off.'

Some people even seemed to support the South African system. Jim Turner's dad told several of us that 'we might have come up with a similar system here if we'd had to live with twenty million Maoris.' Our mothers seemed to agree with most of what their husbands were saying. Or if they didn't, they kept their opinions to themselves.

Not everyone down the Spit was against the march that was planned for the eighth of June. Matt Templeton's sisters were all for it. Matt reported to us that all five of the older ones had announced their intention to go, even though their father had strictly forbidden it. Matt said there had been several blazing rows and two of his sisters were now living in the sleep-out at the back of the section, coming inside to eat only when their father was out of the house.

Another person who made it clear that she was against the tour was Mrs Montgomery. She was a widow who lived only a few doors down from the Ashers' dairy. For reasons beyond us, she had sellotaped a copy of the poster advertising the rally up in her front window so that it was visible from the road. Widow makes her sound old but actually she was only in her early forties. Mr Montgomery had died of a sniping stroke that hit him at the age of thirty-seven. He had been out on the street staining his front fence. When he was found he had lain in the pool of spilt timber-stain long enough for his left hand and half his face to be stained a deep brown. They kept the casket closed at the funeral. The joke that quickly did the rounds was that Mr Montgomery had looked like he was a Maori. 'Or at least half Maori!'

Right up until the tour ended Mrs Montgomery wore one of those HART badges. We knew for a fact that on one occasion the local post-master had refused to serve her while she had the badge on. Mrs Montgomery had told him that in that case she would get her stamps elsewhere. But along with the Templeton girls, she was in the minority. Most people in New Brighton regarded the planned march as being outside the boundaries of what was acceptable. We had even heard it talked about as being the act of traitors.

In early May Mr Templeton was still giving Jim Turner a hard time during rugby training. Apart from lacking the requisite killer instinct, Jim didn't have good enough fitness levels, said his coach. In fairness, it wasn't just Jim he was picking on. The first XV had lost the first three games of the season and Mr Templeton was ratcheting up the pressure on all his players. The upcoming tour made performing well seem even more important than in a normal season. Jim responded by running in the sand hills six days a week. He also started eating a lot of eggs and bananas. He had read somewhere that they were good for athletes who wanted to lift their performance. And running through sand hills is about the best exercise there is for building up stamina. The soft sand is murder on the legs and after a few minutes of that, guys who think they are fit find that their thighs are on fire and they're breathing like steam trains. It's no exaggeration that after a month of regular running on the dunes, Jim Turner found running around the rugby field for eighty minutes to be a piece of piss.

It was a Saturday morning and the sea fog had laid itself down over the Spit again. It didn't bother Jim, though. He only needed to see as far as his next footfall. He had run through the dunes from his parents' place up to the playground with the swimming pool that's close to the shopping centre. The pool still has a concrete whale sitting in the middle. The whale is painted blue at the start of each summer and when there's water in the pool the blowhole is a fountain. We all have memories of climbing the whale as kids, and sliding down its back into the water. These days there is a new pier close to the playground and a flash library with two cafés and outdoor seating. But back then there was just a slide, and the whale pool and swings over concrete.

Jim had stopped to stretch before turning back. He was leaning against the wall of the changing rooms, pushing against it with one leg straight behind him, when he heard a weird sound, 'like someone drowning and crying at the same time'. The fog was drifting in banks that shifted and then melted back together, creating small rooms that gave way to bigger spaces and then closed in again.

Jim stood near the edge of the swimming pool. With summer over, the big concrete whale was chipped and faded. The pool had been drained but had filled up again with rainwater that had turned green and been fouled by the seagulls that gathered around its edges to drink. Curious, Jim walked up the steps to the car park. There were a few surfers' cars, parked mostly at the front where, on a clear day, you could check out the waves. Some people will surf in any weather as long as the waves are good. To Jim they sounded big as they broke but he couldn't see them through the fog. The surfers must have all been out because he could see no one sitting in any of the cars. It was a large car park and the vehicles down the other end drifted in and out of view.

And then he heard the noise again. 'The second time it sounded to me like a hurt animal, a dog or something. It was coming from an old dunger; a surfer's car but with the board still strapped to the roof-rack.'

Jim approached cautiously and peered into the rear window. A second later he was pulling the back door open and ripping a guy out backwards by his hair. The guy's jeans were around his ankles and his cock stirred the foggy air in front of him. Jim may have lacked the killer instinct but he was still a big guy. He was used to the push and shove, the gouge and jab of the scrum and the maul, the sharp toe of the ruck. Plus he had the element of surprise. The guy he was holding by the hair was a surfer who lived up North New Brighton. His family was Catholic and he went to the school next to the basilica in the city, where he was in his final year. He was not on our list. Jim let go of the guy's hair. While he was still trying to find his footing Jim put both hands on the guy's chest and shoved as hard as he could, which was pretty hard. The guy's pants were still around his ankles and he tumbled backwards on to the concrete.

Jim told us that the surfer started to roll away, at the same time pulling at his pants, which were prevented from coming off by his shoes. He was yelling, pretty generic abuse, but Jim distinctly heard him say, 'She wanted me to. She said she liked it.'

Jim dropped his hands to his side. The guy had time to stagger to his feet where he swayed like a Weeble. 'Fuck off,' Jim said.

'What about my car?'

'Fuck off,' Jim said again and took a couple of steps forward. Apparently, the guy didn't argue. He simply pulled up his jeans and sloped off into the fog where he could be seen sitting sullenly by the changing rooms.

Of course the girl in the car was Carolyn Asher. By then she was sitting up in the back seat, her feet dangling out the open door. She was naked except for a white bra. 'What did you do that for?' she asked. Jim said that she didn't seem angry, or even surprised. She was just asking.

'I thought he was hurting you.'

One of Carolyn's long, pale hands went to her neck, where fresh bruises were already rising to the surface of her skin.

'Help me find my clothes.'

In the end Jim settled for standing awkwardly near the car while Carolyn dressed. When he finally looked at her, she was wearing a white dress with a frilled hem, and a pale pink sweater. They looked to Jim like the clothes she would have worn to go out the night before. She asked him to help her tie her shoe and put her leg up on the bumper of the car. 'Come on,' she said when he had finished.

'What about him?' asked Jim. The Catholic surfer was still standing by the changing room, staring in their direction.

'He'll live,' was all Carolyn said. She took Jim by the hand and walked with him towards the road.

They continued hand in hand through the fog. Occasionally cars came by, driving slowly with their headlights on. To the drivers Jim and Carolyn must have looked like a young couple who, bored with being cooped up inside, had gone for a walk in the fog. Jim said that he didn't know what to say so he kept quiet. He could see where the sun was supposed to be, a yellowing in a patch of sky, but no warmth broke through the ceiling of fog. They walked as far as Bridge Street before Carolyn spoke. Jim had to lean close to hear her.

'So what have you guys found out?'

'About what?'

'You're one of those guys trying to find out who killed my sister. Come on, I'm not stupid.'

He didn't bother denying it on our behalf. 'Nothing much.'

142

She shook her head. 'I don't think they're ever going to catch him.'

There was, he said, a sadness to her; what in later years we could have labelled as fatalism. No more was said. They walked on through the fog until they came to the Ashers' dairy. The closed sign was still in the window even though it was almost mid-morning.

Carolyn was still holding Jim's hand when she asked him his name. He told her and she repeated it, and smiled for the first time.

'Looks like the fog might clear soon,' was all he could find to say.

'Sure,' she said. Jim was disappointed when she gave his hand a gentle squeeze and finally let it go. Carolyn turned and walked through the gate.

It would be nice to say that big Jim Turner's friendship saved Carolyn Asher, but by that time Carolyn was probably beyond saving, by one of us anyway.

Over the following months she continued diligently working her way through her list, although often we failed to see what light she hoped to throw on the case with some of her choices. The guys seemed to be getting older and not all of them even lived down New Brighton. Carolyn took to wearing shirts with high collars all the time.

Jim sat and passed his driver's licence. He would drive Carolyn around to wherever she wanted to go. She would call him at all hours of the night and he would borrow his older brother's little red Suzuki and meet her outside the dairy. Often she asked him to take her to the flat of some guy she was seeing, though she often didn't stay for long. Jim didn't mind waiting in the car. There was a tape deck and he would sit and listen to Duran Duran or Bowie over and over again. He told us that Carolyn had started smoking, and not just cigarettes: a guy who lived over in Linwood had got her into it.

Carolyn apparently liked being high. She kept seeing that guy for longer than any of the others, possibly because he grew his own in a glasshouse out the back of his flat and had a seemingly endless supply. When she did stop seeing him she would ask Jim to drive her to different places just to buy dope. Some of them had concrete-block fences out the front and barbed wire running around the top. Carolyn would ring the bell and go inside. Jim waited in the car and tried not to ask himself how she was paying.

As they drove around they would talk. Sometimes she was high and her ideas circled slowly around the car like the poems we were still finding blowing on the wind. Jim told us that she liked to talk about Lucy. 'Lots of little things that she remembered from when they were young and stuff.'

Of course the rest of us couldn't help wondering if Jim and Carolyn were sleeping together. It was hard

'Lots of little things that she remembered from when they were young and stuff.'

Of course the rest of us couldn't help wondering if Jim and Carolyn were sleeping together. It was hard for us to imagine just talking about stuff with a girl like Carolyn Asher had become. But we knew better than to ask Jim for details. All he ever told us about what they talked about, and about what they did when they were alone, was that it was private and that they were good friends.

A couple of other things happened around that time that are worth mentioning. The first has to do with the dead dog.

There is a colony of godwits that arrives at the Spit every spring. Some people make a pretty big deal about it. Apparently the birds fly all the way from Siberia non-stop before gliding in low over the roofs of the houses on Rocking Horse Road and touching down in the reserve at the end of the Spit. They spend the summer feeding in the estuary and then in April or May fly all the way back to Siberia. If you were into birds, flying all that way is a pretty amazing accomplishment, but frankly, at fifteen we couldn't have cared less. To us the godwits were just little speckled birds with long legs, not all that different from the other wading birds who lived in the estuary year-round.

We only got interested because that year something started killing them. One morning in April a research student from the university found about a Society types with beards, hanging around discussing the possibility of putting up a temporary fence around where the godwits nested. We were disappointed that the bodies had been cleaned up.

Apart from a few feathers there was nothing to see.

One of the bearded guys came over to us. 'Are you kids local?' We didn't like being called kids but we nodded. He asked if any of us had seen a strange dog hanging around in the last couple of days. We said that we hadn't, which was the truth. Grant told him that people were always walking their dogs up and down the beach.

'No, I mean a dog with no owner, especially in the evening.' As the guy spoke, he looked up and down the beach as though the dog he was talking about might appear at any moment and begin ripping apart more birds. But we'd seen nothing like that. We didn't tell him but we knew that with all the dunes and lupins a dog could move around in the reserve for days pretty much unseen.

Two days later, *The Press* reported on page two that the killer had struck again. This time three birds were dead. Another two godwits were being treated by a local vet for serious injuries and were not expected to survive. We were looking for a distraction from school and from the Asher case, so when Tug Gardiner suggested we build a trap for the killer dog, everyone was keen.

We raided our fathers' garages and sheds and that afternoon carried a selection of spades and shovels down to the reserve. We chose a spot in the dip behind the first dune, about a hundred metres from where the godwits roosted. There was a thin track used by rabbits where we had previously had some luck laying makeshift snares. A dog, however, is a lot bigger than a rabbit and we knew that catching one would require more than a snare made out of string.

There were five of us there that afternoon and we dug a fair-sized hole. It was about two metres square and three metres deep, with sheer sides. It was hard work. After we had finished digging we collected long, thin bits of driftwood and placed then in a rough lattice over the top of the hole. Using the edges of the spades we then hacked down lupins and laid the branches over the top of the sticks. The lupins bled milky white and our hands became sticky as we worked.

Roy Moynahan had thought to bring some bait. His mother had made a roast chook for dinner the night before and Roy had brought the carcass wrapped in newspaper. He unwrapped it and tossed the bones down the hole. Then we covered the last gap in the top with more lupins.

We returned the next morning before school. It had rained hard in the night and the sand had a dark crust that our footsteps broke through and shattered. We thought that the rain would have spoiled our chances of catching anything but from a distance we could see that something had collapsed the sticks and lupins covering the hole. When we knelt down and peered into the shadows we saw two things we were not expecting. The first was that the hole was half full of water. The tide was still high, and it had raised the water-table to above the bottom of our hole. Sea water had oozed up through the sand and into the hole, where it had mixed with the rain water from the night before. The second thing was that we had caught a dog, a small tan-and-white thing that Al Penny identified as a Jack Russell. The body of the dog floated side by side with the chicken carcass. The fat from the chicken had made a shiny smear over the surface of the water.

If a larger dog had fallen into our hole, it would have been tall enough to stand on the bottom with its head above the water level. But a Jack Russell has short legs. You could see the scratch marks where it had tried to scramble up the side of the hole but the sand must've kept collapsing back on it. Eventually it would have become too tired to swim any more and drowned.

Al raised the point, how did we even know this was the dog that had killed the birds? The truth was we had no idea. It was probably just somebody's pet. The trap now seemed like a stupid idea, dangerous and irresponsible, even childish.

Mark Murray got down in the hole and fished out the body. His parents had always owned dogs, and he was used to them, although he said he had never lifted a dead one before and was surprised at how heavy it was. Mark laid the body on a patch of tussock so that it didn't get sand stuck to its fur. Its legs were stiff and its body hard to the touch as though it had never been a real, living thing but had been construct-ed from fibreglass in someone's shed. The dog had a fierce look on its face. Its gums were drawn back from its teeth and its glassy eyes were open as though it had tried to stare death down.

Of course we covered up the hole so that no other animals—or worse, some small kid—would fall into it (why hadn't that occurred to us before?). We had no shovels this time so we used our hands and it took us a fair while. Then we buried the dog. We stood around the grave and there was an embarrassed si-lence. We were already late for school but sensed that something should be said or done. Eventually Roy Moynahan spoke. He talked to the dog as if it could still hear us, mostly about how we were sorry we'd killed him and how we hadn't meant to. 'I hope that there's a dog heaven,' he said. 'And that you've got everything you want there.' And then we left for school, shuffling through the dunes to where our bikes were.

About a week later a handmade poster went up in the supermarket with a picture of the dog we'd drowned. Apparently, its name was Mac and a reward was offered for its safe return. We never did call the number. How do you explain to someone that you've trapped and drowned their dog? We all agreed that it was better Mac's owners thought it had simply wandered away. At least then they were left with the hope that their dog had been found by a nice family. The parents could pretend to their kids that Mac was living the good life somewhere with two or three pet-mad kids who slipped him food under the table every night and walked him twice a day.

Our only consolation was that after that morning there were no more attacks on the godwits. Still, we felt bad about the whole thing.

The other incident that should get a mention is what the papers called 'The third sex attack in the South Brighton area within three months' *(The Press, p1, May 11, 1981).* If we're clearing the air then we might as well put down what we know about that as well.

For several weeks, Matt Templeton had been carrying messages between his sister, Mary-Rose, and a boy called Brent Cox. In '81 Mary-Rose was a year above us at school; in what was then the seventh form. Brent Cox was nineteen and worked at the local garage as an apprentice car mechanic. We all agreed that they were a good match. Both of them were generally acknowledged to be good-looking. Also, both Mary-Rose and Brent had the intellectual and social laziness that beautiful people can often get away with. They both drifted through life on their looks. Not that they were bad people. We all agreed that they were just a bit up themselves.

Matt was on to a good little earner with Brent. The guy was sending one or two notes a day to Mary-Rose and they were meeting pretty regularly. Luckily Mr Templeton was distracted by the first XV's poor performance. In addition to running the history department he was now holding training twice a week and keeping the team out to all hours. The players hated it but Matt's sisters were thrilled. The long summer holidays where their father hung around the house were hell for them. Things had, of course, been worse after the attack on their sister's friend—and now there was the family friction over the upcoming Springbok tour.

But the Templeton girls could get away with a lot more during that winter. Matt's mum was relatively easy to fool no matter what the season. With seven children, all still at home, Mrs Templeton permanently wore the dazed expression of a veteran of the trenches.

One evening in the Turners' garage, Matt told a few of us that after dinner Mary-Rose had been secretly meeting Brent Cox at the surf club, which was only a few minutes' walk along the road from the Templetons' house. Mary-Rose would tell her parents that she was going to her room to do her homework and then slip out the window. She would only go for about half an hour. Matt or her sisters would cover for her, if necessary. But with so many people in the house, one more or less was unlikely to be no- ticed—not in the short term.

A few evenings later, with nothing better to do, Grant Webb, Pete Marshall and Jase Harbidge went down to the surf club. They camped in the dunes at an elevated spot, and waited. Their motivations were mixed. We all suspected what Mary-Rose and Brent were doing at the surf club and the idea of catching a glimpse of them at it caused a tingling knot of excitement in our guts. Grant had his own reason for being there. He been pushed around by Brent Cox and a couple of Brent's mates at the start of the third form. It had been nothing too serious, just your garden-variety bullying that didn't last more than a couple of weeks, but the idea of some kind of payback was undoubtedly in Grant's mind.

About half an hour after they got there, Mary-Rose arrived. They watched her walk beneath the two car park lights. She was looking around furtively as she hurried across the open space. As Jase said later, 'The way she was acting, even a blind man would be suspicious.'

The surf club has two levels: below the large open hall where the life guards hang out is a storage area where the two surfboats, the surf-skis and all the rest of the equipment are stored. To get in underneath there were two doors, which swung outwards on tracks. These days there is a metal roller-door but back then the doors had wooden slats. They were split down the middle and swung outwards so that there was enough room to wheel the boats through. Normally the doors were bolted top and bottom and padlocked shut but apparently Brent Cox had a key. When Mary-Rose knocked and called his name, one door was pushed open slightly from the inside, and Mary-Rose disappeared inside.

Grant and Pete and Jase waited a while but nothing happened. They began to get cold. Jase later admitted suggesting that they slide the bolt on the door home and then wait to see what happened. Grant said that he had a better idea. The three of them crept down to the door of the storage area. Mary-Rose had pulled it shut after her and Pete had to lift the heavy door so that it didn't scrape on the concrete pad.

It was almost totally dark. The last daylight came through the slats in the door and they could just make out the outlines of the two surf-boats. Luckily Brent and Mary-Rose had chosen to go right down the back. The three guys could faintly hear them whispering. They crouched perfectly still and waited for their eyes to adjust. After a few minutes Grant gestured for Pete and Jase to stay where they were and then he slipped away.

Jase and Pete stood and listened to the sounds coming from the back of the big open space. Mary-Rose had stopped giggling. There was another, deeper sound now. As Pete stood and listened uncomfortably, he realised that the sound was Brent Cox grunting deep in his throat, like a pig. Pete admitted to some of us later that he started to feel bad about being there. He expected at any moment for there to be a shout and for Brent to come charging out of the darkness after Grant, pissed off as all hell. But for what seemed to him to be a very long time there was only the darkness and the animal sounds.

And then Grant suddenly appeared next to them like a genie out of a bottle. They could see that he was grinning in the darkness, his teeth white. He had a bundle in his arms. Grant held one finger to his lips and gestured. The three of them slipped out the door and returned to their observation post in the dunes where Grant showed the other two what he had got. Of course, it was Brent Cox's clothes, his jeans, inside which nestled a pair of white jockeys, and his sweat shirt. There was no sign of his shoes or socks. Grant also had Mary-Rose's dress. Grant admitted that he had been hoping to get a pair of trousers at best but Mary-Rose had folded all the clothes up and put them on the edge of a surf-boat, a short distance from where she and Brent were lying on a pile of life-jackets. All Grant had to do was reach out and take them.

'Did you see anything?' Jase wanted to know.

'Just Cox's white arse going up and down.'

They waited, shivering in the cold. Pete said that he could smell the scent of Mary-Rose on the dress, as though the printed flowers that covered it were giving off a perfume. When Mary-Rose's half hour was almost up they heard whispers coming from the shed and the sound of things being moved around. Brent Cox was clearly heard to say, 'Well, you better bloody find them!' A few more minutes passed during which the whispers became louder and more panicked.

Apparently Mary-Rose feared being discovered missing by her father more than any embarrassment.

She finally appeared at the door in nothing but her bra, knickers, shoes and socks. After a hurried look around, she set off at a trot in the direction of her house. Brent Cox could be heard hissing after her, telling her to bring him back some clothes. But apparently he had no faith that Mary-Rose would return with something for him to wear. He also appeared at the door and set off after her. Apart from his shoes and socks he was naked and must have been freezing. His only covering was a child-sized life-jacket, which he clutched to his groin with both hands. Brent's parents' house was in the same direction as the Templetons' but at least a couple of k's further down the road. Maybe he figured he could steal some pants from a clothesline on the way or that Mary-Rose would pass him something from her window.

Needless to say this was better than even Grant Webb had imagined. The three guys were killing themselves up in the dunes as Brent took off after Mary-Rose, clutching his orange life-jacket to his groin, and running with the bent-over lope of someone lower down the evolutionary scale.

That was the picture that the community patrol saw as they pulled into the car-park: A girl, stripped to her underwear, being chased by a naked guy, clutching something to his groin. To a group of guys cruising the neighbourhood looking for a sexual predator, you have to admit Brent Cox more than fitted the description.

The car was being driven by Mr Erickson, a retired stevedore. Old Erickson didn't hesitate. He gunned the motor and drove right at Brent. Pete later swore to us that he was sure Erickson was intending to run the guy down. But Brent heard the surge of the engine and saw the danger in time. He swerved away from the middle of the car park towards the retaining wall on the beach side. As he came to it he dropped the life-jacket. He vaulted the low wall and hit the sand running. Apart from his shoes and socks he was now completely naked.

It sounds funny to tell it, like a scene out of *The Benny Hill Show,* but Pete and Jase and Grant realised the seriousness of the situation straight away. The guys in Erickson's car thought they were after a child molester and possibly a murderer. They weren't pissing about. They were already spilling out even before the car had come to a complete stop. One of them, turned out to be Jim Mr Turner's dad. He immediately gave chase along the beach. The other two ran to the back of the car where they hauled up the boot and snatched up torches and a couple of softball bats, and then they ran after Brent as well.

As Grant said later that evening, 'Cox is a bit of a prick, but I didn't want him to be beaten to death.' And he wasn't exaggerating the danger for once. After Lucy's murder, and then the attack on the two young girls, people down on the Spit were edgy. Men were quicker to shout. Neighbours had begun arguing about small things; autumn bonfires and barking dogs. Our dads were drinking more beer in the evenings and at the weekends. A few of our fathers had been in fights lately, mostly about the Springbok tour. The atmosphere was brittle. People were itching to take action but they didn't know what to do. Erickson and the other men in the car had probably been drinking and if they caught Brent you could guarantee they'd be using their fists and the bats, long before they asked any questions. Looking back it's clear that the community patrol was as much about the hope of delivering Old Testament vengeance as it was about keeping the streets safe.

Luckily, in all the confusion, Mary-Rose had vanished into the darkness of the sand dunes in the direction of the road. Mr Erickson had a bad knee. He stayed with the car, keeping the engine running. He was craning his neck and peering around as though expecting more naked perverts to appear at any minute. Grant, Pete and Jase skirted the back of the surf club, keeping out of Erickson's sight. They walked along the road in the direction Brent had gone and then cut down a little-used track to the beach. They found Mr Turner standing on the beach staring up into the dunes, a torch in his hand. Shouts came from the two other men and they could be heard thrashing through the lupin. The beams of their torches darted here and there. Apparently Brent Cox had gone to ground. The three guys imagined him lying, naked, scared and as cold as hell, in a hollow among the tussock plants somewhere close by.

Mr Turner was too worked up to question why three friends of his son were down on the beach at that hour.

'Have you boys seen anyone, a guy running?'

Pete looked down the beach towards the surf club. 'We just saw a naked guy. Back down that way. He ran out of the dunes and went down the road.'

Mr Turner swore loudly and called to the other men. They immediately returned sliding down the face of the first dune. The three of them ran back up the beach. Jase and Pete and Grant stood watching until the men disappeared from sight. Over the sound of the waves they heard Erickson's car reversing quickly and driving away.

Jase put the bundle of clothes he was carrying, including Mary-Rose's dress, down on the sand and called out loudly, 'Hey, Cox! Your clothes are here!' There was no response. Nothing moved in the darkness. So the three of them simply walked away. It was only when they were almost at the surf club that they looked back and saw a furtive shadow come down on to the beach, snatch up the clothes and then dart away back to the relative safety of the dunes.

The community patrol drove up and down Marine Parade as far as the shopping centre but saw nothing. They eventually got around to calling the police. Jase Harbidge's dad got the full story from his mates on the force and we heard the police side of the story from Jase. Two tracking dogs were brought in. The dogs got really excited about a pile of life-jackets in the storage area under the surf club, which had apparently been broken into.

The dogs tracked the scent up the beach and into the dunes where the police discovered the suspect had hidden himself under a hastily made covering of lupin branches. From there the dogs tracked him back to the surf club but lost the scent. He appeared to have left in some type of vehicle (Pete remembered seeing Brent's bicycle chained up next to the outdoor shower).

From the police's point of view, the real mystery was the identity of the third victim. Mr Turner and the other members of the community patrol hadn't been able to identify the girl seen fleeing in her underwear. After a couple of beers at the Empire Mr Erickson would describe her as having 'the type of arse you only dream about'. But luckily for Mary-Rose his description was no more specific than that.

The front-page headline in the nest day's *Press* read NEW BRIGHTON ATTACKS CONTINUE. The accompanying article explained that,

Experts claim it isn't unusual for victims of rape and sexual violence not to come forward immediately. Victims are often embarrassed and ashamed of what has happened to them. Some victims blame themselves for the attack.

Police, however, are calling for the young woman to contact them as soon as possible. A police spokesman said: 'The sooner we talk to this young

woman, the more likely it is we will catch her attacker.'

(Exhibit F78, The Press, *May 12)*

The spokesman also praised the bravery of the four men, who he described as 'driving the attacker away from his intended victim. In all likelihood these men prevented a much more serious crime.' In that day's editorial *The Press* went even further: 'If not for the men's brave intervention, New Brighton could have seen another young girl dead at the hands of the Christmas Killer.'

The week after Brent Cox's streak down the beach, we heard that an arrest had been made in the abduction case. The police in Nelson had questioned a man seen acting suspiciously outside a primary school. According to Bill Harbidge's contact up in Nelson, the interviewing officers had been surprised when, with hardly any prompting, the guy had confessed to the attack on Tracy Templeton and Jenny Jones months before.

He was in his early thirties, a Maori named Wiremu Jones. He confessed with tears pouring down his face. He still wore the dirty hat that Tracy remembered, as he told the police that he had been raised 'a good Christian boy' but that 'the devil has me by the throat'.

There was no need for Tracy or Jenny to sit through a long trial. The guy had confessed and was eventually sentenced to three years in prison.

At fifteen we thought three years was fair, a lifetime.

Since then we've kept track as Wiremu Jones has been in and out of prison like a yo-yo. He got out in late '83 and had only been out for six months when he molested an eleven-year-old in Wellington and ended up going back inside for another seven years. In '97 he was arrested for exposing himself to a busload of school kids on their way back from a trip to Te Papa. In 2000 he tried to entice seven-year-old twin girls into his car in Dunedin. Apparently being locked up together in a chocolate box of murderers, thieves and other perverts has failed to show Wiremu the error of his ways. Or maybe it is just that the devil still has a firm grip on his throat.

Although, God knows, he is guilty of a lot, the police were sure that Wiremu Jones did not murder Lucy Asher. He travelled around a fair bit and in late December of 1980 when Lucy was killed Wiremu was living with a cousin up on the east coast, near Gisborne. He didn't travel down south until almost a month later. As is often the case, our imaginations had taken two similar events and assumed a common cause. One of the things that our investigation has taught us over the years is that life is almost never that simple.

FIVE

Two months after his diagnosis Pete had lost weight. But the truth is that all of us could benefit by losing a bit of weight. Twenty years' worth of beer and easy food have washed up around our middles. By late August last year the flesh had melted away from Pete's belly and from the sag below his jaw. He actually started to look younger, even healthier. To those of us who had known him almost all his life he seemed to be aging backwards. Pete began to look more as he had done in his early thirties and then as the weeks shifted underfoot he regained the taut looks he had possessed during his twenties. By October he again had the wiry frame of the teenage boy who had discovered Lucy Asher's body on the beach.

He was often tired, but the full force of the cancer hadn't yet hit him. That would come soon and when it did it would be unremitting. Pete had taken to rising with the sun as it cracked through the watery curve of the eastern horizon, and going for slow walks that took him all over the Spit. He often stopped and just sat. Pete lived down by the reserve in the single-bedroom unit he'd bought about ten years earlier, with the money left over from his divorce. He and his wife had no kids but between work and us he never seemed to be short of company when he wanted it. When he woke early there was no one to disturb except the ginger tom he had adopted.

On one particular morning—it was the first week in October—he was walking out on the mud-flats of the estuary behind the Spit. 'Mud-flats' is actually not a very accurate description although that's what everyone's always called them. At low tide a lot of the estuary is more sand than mud, coarse and black and pitted with infinite numbers of small crab holes, and graffitied by the swirling trails of cat's-eye shells. It is only truly muddy in patches and it's easy to watch out for those and walk around them. In all the kilometres and kilometres of space the only real obstacles are the braided channels, which are never the same from one day to the next. Even the two or three main channels winding down from the two river-mouths to the end of the Spit where the estuary discharges into the sea, even they shift from season to season. At low tide it's easy to walk around for hours out there. All you really have to remember is to wear a good pair of shoes and to keep one eye on the tide, which can flood back in quickly.

Later, when we were visiting him in the hospital, Pete told us that the pain hit him suddenly. One second he was feeling fine, lost in his thoughts (we didn't have the nerve to ask him what those might have been); the next he was engulfed—'like hot shrapnel had been shot into my gut'. It was as though all the pain he had avoided since his diagnosis had been stored up and then unleashed. As he spoke to us, he moved his legs around under the heavy white hospital sheets.

'The ambulance guy asked me how the pain was on a scale of one to ten. I told him to stop asking me stupid maths questions and to hurry up with the painkillers.'

Some old woman who lived on the estuary side of the Spit had apparently been watching, through binoculars, Pete's progress across the mud-flats. When she saw him clutch his stomach and go down she had immediately called an ambulance. She had declined to give her name. It just goes to show that sometimes even nosy neighbours have their uses.

The ambulance guys had to come across the mudflats on foot. It's a good thing they hurried because the tide was coming in by the time they got to Pete. He was lying in the foetal position and they lifted him out of water that was lapping at his body. They hauled him up moaning and dripping, on to the stretcher. He couldn't move without pain erupting from his guts. He hung between them curled like an ammonite, listening to their voices grumble about their shoes getting wet.

Despite the dramatic nature of his collapse, that first time Pete was admitted to hospital he only stayed in two nights; for observation. They gave him morphine in the ambulance but after about twelve hours the pain subsided of its own accord, although after that it never completely went away and had to be managed continually. Neither the doctors nor Pete (nor even we) were fooled into thinking Pete would go back to the way he had been before.

During his stay in the hospital we all came to visit, although not all together at once; the room was too small. It seemed wrong to turn up empty-handed. Chocolates didn't seem right as a gift. Pete had never had much of a sweet tooth, and he had been off his food for weeks. Flowers were girly. In the end Pete got enough grapes to have his own vintage. He ended up giving most of them away to the three old blokes he shared a room with.

On the evening of that first day in hospital Jase Harbidge found himself alone with Pete. It was long after visiting hours had finished, and dark outside. The three other guys in the room had their curtains pulled around their beds and seemed to be asleep, although you could never really tell. All day we had observed them doze for a while and then their eyelids would suddenly flutter open and they would start forward from their pillows. They would look around as if to reassure themselves that they were still alive. After a few seconds they would lie back with ambivalence—a mixture of relief at being alive and disappointment at the circumstances in which they rediscovered themselves.

The oncology ward is on the top floor of the hospital with views out over the botanical gardens, which at night are just a dark pool surrounded by the city lights. Jase said that the chemical smell of the place seemed to have collected over the day and risen up to where he and Pete were. Pete was still on the morphine then, his voice blurring around the edges of his words. Jase had just got up off his seat to open the window, when Pete spoke.

'I thought I saw her. Out on the flats.'

Jase didn't have to ask who. There was a pause filled only by the sound of the air conditioning and the rattling breath of the dying man in the far corner.

'I thought I saw her walking towards me with the incoming tide. She was walking on the water. But she couldn't get to me before the ambulance guys.' Pete laughed quietly. 'When they picked me up I was so pissed off. I wanted to tell them to leave me for her.'

That was all he said before he fell asleep. Jase sat and watched him sleep for a while and when he was sure that Pete was not going to wake up again he stood, careful not to scrape the foot of his chair on the lino, and left quietly.

During visiting hours the next morning the old man who had slept in the corner bed was gone and Pete had no memory of most of the day before. When we talked about it later we all agreed that it was probably just the morphine talking. It was best not to mention it to Pete again.

In 1981 South Brighton High School ran a system where senior students were given responsibility for various duties around the school. In the second term we sometimes found ourselves rostered to police the queue of refractory third and fourth formers at the canteen. Twice a month, we were expected to stand by the iron gates in front of the school for ten minutes before the first bell and ten minutes after and to write down the names of all latecomers. We enforced silence in the library, and patrolled distant corners of the school grounds where occasionally we would see puffs of white smoke rising up from behind the clumps of ragged hebes like Indian signals.

Another of the duties we had was working in Lost and Found. Stray jackets and bags, books and pencil cases—named and unnamed—were all deposited in a room little bigger than a large wardrobe between the boys' lockers and the library. For everyone who had lost something over the week, Lost and Found was their first port of call. Every Wednesday, whoever was on duty was excused from the last morning lesson five minutes early so that they could get the key from its hook inside the door of the staff room. We were supposed to have Lost and Found open by the time the lunch bell rang.

It wasn't quite as mindless as it sounds because the job involved handling money. To reclaim an item cost twenty cents. Whoever was rostered on had to collect the float from the teacher on duty and record how much was paid in (some kids reclaimed more than one item), who it came from, and what it was they had collected. The small float was so you could give change. The theory was that having to pay to get your stuff back (and only being able to get it back once a week) would discourage carelessness. In practice, losing stuff was habitual. The same kids turned up each week looking for their things. Often the same bag or pencil case moved between its owner and Lost and Found with the instincts of a homing pigeon. Some items had been known to be retrieved by their owner at lunchtime, and go back to Lost and Found before school finished that same day.

Mark Murray didn't mind when it was his turn in Lost and Found. It was the second Wednesday in May. He had collected two dollars and forty cents by a quarter to one, and was thinking of closing up early so that he could get a pie from the canteen, when a fourth form girl turned up. We don't have a record of her name but Mark described her as being pale and scrawny with long black hair parted down the middle. 'She was like that girl from *The Munsters,'* he said (although that was a bit rich coming from a guy whose own hair had earned him the nickname Afro Man). The girl informed Mark that she was looking for a jacket lost around October the previous year. When he asked her why she hadn't come to look for it earlier, she eyed him like he was an idiot. 'It was summer and I didn't need it, did I? Now it's cold.'

Items were tossed into Lost and Found without reference to any system. The most recent finds tended to be at the front. Looking further back turned you into an archaeologist: you had to dig back through layers laid down over weeks and months. The only clean-out was done when Lost and Found provided stock for the school fair's white elephant stall, last held in '78. Mark didn't know where to start. Some jackets and umbrellas hung from a hook behind the door but some had fallen on the floor. The girl had described her jacket as being black. With her peering over his shoulder, Mark picked up the top jacket on the floor and then another and another. There were three unclaimed bags under there as well; these he pushed aside. Lying next to them, half covered by a fallen raincoat, was a canvas duffel bag that Mark recognised straight away. It was army-green with two strings through which Lucy used to hook her arm so that the bag dangled from her shoulder. Lucy had scribbled over the canvas in pen and there was a large red peace symbol sewn on the front.

Mark told the girl to wait outside and when she sullenly moved away he opened the bag. Inside was a can of Coke, a small box of tampons (which made Mark uncomfortable), two French textbooks and a book on photography long overdue from the public library, with a naked black woman on the front. At the very bottom of the bag was a small blue notebook with a cardboard cover. It was held together by a yellow ribbon. On the cover it said, **LUCY A. PRIVATE!** The letters had been so deeply overwritten in black pen that you could read the words with just your fingertips.

'So is it there or not?'

'What?'

'My jacket.'

'No. Sorry.'

The girl gave him a curious look. 'You okay?'

'Sure. Yeah. Fine.'

She shook her head. 'Mum's going to bloody kill me.' Mark didn't bother replying and she turned and walked away.

Lucy Asher's diary lay on the pool table, lit only by the beam of Jim Turner's torch. The circle of light surrounding it shook slightly. Whether Jim's hand was unsteady from excitement or from the strain of keeping the torch still was impossible to tell. It was nine o'clock at night and dark outside. A gentle rain began to fall on the tar-seal of Rocking Horse Road. As we stood in the garage we could hear the low waves mutter against the beach on the other side of the Spit. Aslan, the black Alsatian across at number sixty-seven, had barked himself hoarse earlier than usual that night and was sending rasping coughs into the world outside his gate.

We had waited until everyone could get there. Several of us were wearing our pyjamas under our clothes. Al Penny wore tartan slippers belonging to his father. Tug Gardiner had on a sweatshirt with a hood that, for some reason, he had pulled up over his head, but we were in too serious a mood to question him. The news of Mark's find had travelled from one of us to another; from house to house like a moth in the night. Jim had had to wait until after rugby training and then a late dinner, during which his mother had tried to talk to him. We had feigned sleepiness and gone to our rooms early, only to slip away through back doors and open windows. The moon was unaccounted for as we slipped through the darkness. We were the furtive noises in the night.

It was Pete Marshall who broke the spell. He carefully lifted the book off the green felt. Perhaps, because he had been the one who found Lucy's body, Pete felt he had a special right, or possibly an obligation. The ribbon resisted him but at last succumbed to his fumbling and he opened the cover to view the first page of the diary of Lucy Asher. Jim held the torch higher so that the narrow beam of light spilled over Pete's shoulder and on to the first page.

Although we have all handled the book and read its contents more than once in the years since then, only Pete has ever read it aloud. By being the first to intone Lucy's words he became, in a sense, her voice. He read well, right from that first night. Pete instinctively knew not to try to imitate a young woman's voice nor to attempt dramatic emphasis. He kept his voice neutral, clear and slow, which allowed us to hear within it Lucy's own. All the drama we needed was there in the words.

The diary starts on Lucy's seventeenth birthday, May the twenty-ninth, seven months before she died. There is an inscription on the inside cover —*To Lucyloo from Dad.* To the uninitiated the details might seem mundane, even trivial, but we were teenagers and in the grip of something huge and powerful that held us tightly, even jealously. All that year it had shaken us awake in the morning and had laid us down in our beds at night. It muttered from the dark corners of our rooms as we tossed and turned. It is enough to say that we hung on every word Pete read.

*May 29: Mum won't let me go out with Sarah and Megan tonight!!! She says I have to stay here for a **FAMILY DINNER.** Sarah says Mum still treats me like a baby because I'm the eldest and I only have a sister. She's allowed out because she has four older brothers and her parents are too tired to care. If only my parents were Catholics too and not boring old Presbyterians who are allowed to use a rubber. Worse luck me.*

June 2: Bought the latest Bowie album. It's great. David's hair looks great on the cover. Still too cold to swim. Can't wait for weather to get warmer. Read in the Woman's Weekly that lemon juice in your hair makes it lighter. Have been doing it every night but not sure if it's working. Mum wanted to know where all the lemons from the shop were going. Have to be more careful about what I pinch.

Lucy did not write in her diary every day. Many pages were tantalisingly blank or contained nothing but absent-minded scrawls; swirling labyrinths from which there was no way in or out. Pete held these out in the gloom for us to peer at. Some days she wrote only a couple of words. 'Weather crap' is a typical entry (August 21). The first reference to SJ is on June the thirteenth.

Met SJ in town today. He was shopping for a shirt by himself. Really weird to see him doing something so normal. I saw him before he saw me. I almost kept on walking but soooo glad I didn't. He asked if I'd like to have tea with him at the Ballantynes' tea room. Almost said no but he's really easy to talk to. Keep thinking about him. He has really nice teeth.

June 20: SJ smiled at me today but didn't stop to talk because he was walking with some of the others.

July 16: Some little twerp spilled chocolate milk in the shop the other day and most of it must have gone under the fridge. Now it smells DISGUSTING! Mum blames me for not cleaning it up properly.

August 7: School holidays. Haven't seen SJ for days and days. Feeling sad and lonely which is silly because we hardly ever talk anyway. Think he might have gone away with his family. Mum really being a pain. Might kill myself. [Then in differently coloured pen] *THAT WAS A JOKE! HA HA*

The batteries in Jim's torch were fading fast. As Pete read, the light dimmed until the book was almost indistinguishable from the darkness in the garage. Pete's voice stayed clear and steady but he leaned further and further forward so that by the last few pages he seemed to be about to devour the diary.

*September 14: Played tennis with Sarah today. She **thrashed** me—as usual. Feel bad about not telling her what's been going on but SJ has made me promise not to say a word. He's right that people wouldn't understand about our friendship. Taking the bus into town to meet wouldn't understand about our friendship. Taking the bus into town to meet him* *again today. Think Mum might be getting suspicious about all the time I'm taking off from the shop. Had a big fight about it. Think she's been nosing around in my room. Will take this diary with me to school from now on. Too dangerous here.*

September 28: SJ invited me back to his house tonight after softball practice. Of course we had to go separately. It wasn't like how I imagined it. I thought he'd have heaps of books and stuff like that but he's hardly got any. HE KISSED ME!!!!!! About time. I liked it apart from the way he got a bit rough at the end before I said I had to go. Good that I did leave and not just for the obvious reason. Mum freaked out anyway when I got home because she said anything could have happened to me biking home in the dark. Had another big argument so I'm writing this in my room instead of having dinner. Had some poached eggs and toast at SJ's anyway but Mum doesn't know that. Hope she thinks I'm starving.

P.S. Kissing S was not at all like kissing Phil. Don't know if I should go back.

And then Lucy seemed to lose interest in the diary. October and November were mostly blank. The last entry was on the thirtieth of November, about three weeks before Lucy was murdered and around the time school finished for the year. It was a list of Christmas presents to buy for her family and friends. SJ was not mentioned. Only two were crossed off; a book called *The Painted Years* for her dad and lavender soap for her mother.

It took Pete just under half an hour to read the entire diary aloud. His last words hung in the air and then drifted away through the cracks in the garage walls. We stood in the quarter-light of the dying torch and listened to Aslan coughing. We looked everywhere but at each other. We did not want to see each other's faces; to see written there our own feelings, which we did not have the experience to pin down with names. We were uncertain if men could even speak to each other of such things. We just stood there lost in our thoughts. In that way our emotions were stillborn in the darkness—unnamed and unembraced.

Eventually three white candles were rummaged up from a box in the corner. They were placed in old tin cans on the bench that had become our shrine to Lucy, and solemnly lit. The diary was carefully arranged so that it sat propped up immediately below the photo of Lucy. The three flames danced in the cross-draughts and in the ebb and flow of our breaths. The flickering light reflected off the glass in the photo frame and off Lucy's trophy. The running girl seemed to move; dipping even lower as she crossed the finishing line, and then springing forward and up in triumph.

It is impossible to say when the first of us slipped out of the garage that evening and it has never been established who was the last. Each of us knew when our time came to leave; to say goodnight to Lucy and to slip silently away. Tug Gardiner was still in his dark cowl. Al Penny's overlarge slippers flip-flopped on the concrete path. Jim Turner reported that, from his room, he could see the candles flickering through the cracks in the garage walls until they burnt out just before dawn.

It would be safe to assume that none of us slept that night. How could we? We lay in our beds wrapped in our thoughts. Who among us did not stare into the hollow space above his bed and, with the white noise of the waves whispering suggestions in his ear, try to put a face to the initials SJ?

SIX

We spent the rest of May going over all aspects of Lucy's life, hoping to shed light on the identity of SJ. None of the guys we had on our photo wall had those initials. There *was* one person who lived in the area, Steven Jones, but he was nine years old, and what we called in those days a mongol. There were three other Stephens in the South Brighton area and at least another dozen boys whose name started with a hiss and a twist. But we knew we were clutching at straws. It wasn't proof of anything to be called Stephen or Stuart, Jamison or Johnstone.

As we racked our brains, even we couldn't help noticing that the anti-tour movement was growing stronger. It began to dominate the *Six O'Clock News* and the papers. Someone had the bright idea of telling everyone who was opposed to the tour to leave their taps running. It became commonplace to walk into a public toilet and find all the taps jammed on full, the water swirling away down the basins, the white noise hissing like an angry possum in the small concrete room. Outside taps were also targeted. Everywhere water was left running. We thought it was ridiculous. What did they hope to gain by wasting all that water? We turned taps off when we found them but when we came back again they would be twisted on even harder. After a while we gave up and just ignored them until a back-ground of running water became normal.

One evening the Prime Minister came on the telly to make an announcement about the Springbok tour. His broadcast had been well advertised and people were keen to hear what he had to say. In everyone's homes the sets were on ready to hear the special telecast. Later we heard that a million New Zealanders watched him that night. We knew that our fathers didn't like Muldoon. The man they called Piggy, Piggy Muldoon. They hadn't voted for his National Party, which was the party of farmers and business owners But they still sat on the couch and nodded along with what he said.

'Apartheid—the vast majority of New Zealanders abhor it, like racial discrimination everywhere. But need we hate the South Africans taken one by one? The government will not order the Rugby Union to abandon the tour. The issue now rests with the New Zealand Rugby Union. I say to them, think well before you make your decision.'

Most people down the Spit agreed that this was fair enough. Sport was sport and politics was something else. Muldoon had also made a good point when he said that New Zealanders and South Africans had fought together in the war. Only Jase's dad seemed doubtful. Bill Harbidge rarely drank any more and had lost weight. Jase told us that his dad was punching the bag for half an hour in the garage every evening. He was even cooking dinner for Jase and his sister a few times a week. After Muldoon's broadcast he turned off the television. 'The Rugby Union isn't going to call it off.' He shook his head. 'It's going to be a bloody mess.' The next morning Bill Harbidge got up early, put on his uniform and reported back for work.

The week after that, all the letterboxes on Rocking Horse Road were stuffed with instructions for how to make a Molotov cocktail. The sheets of white A4 paper nestled up to the supermarket flyers and coupon books. The newspaper reported that identical flyers had been appearing in various suburbs of the city over the last week. The police wanted to talk to the people responsible. Anyone with information was urged to come forward. But in the end no one was caught.

We were interested to see it isn't that hard to make a Molotov cocktail. According to the instructions, anyway. You fill up a glass bottle with petrol and then stick a rolled-up rag in the top. Apparently you have to make sure that the rag is pushed down into the petrol before you light it. Otherwise the fuel might not catch when the bottle is thrown.

No one was sure if the instructions were printed by a group who thought Molotov cocktails might be useful in stopping the tour, or being spread by tour supporters who imagined walls of flame holding back those intent on stopping the rugby.

On the evening of the anti-tour march, we all rode our bikes up to Thompson Park to have a look. Even though our parents had forbidden us from going anywhere near, you couldn't have kept us away.

As it turned out, it wasn't the big show that we thought it was going to be. A stage, just a few wooden boxes really, had been set up close to the road where the street lights lit the edge of the park at night. A young woman in a long purple dress was testing the microphone when we arrived. It was after six o'clock and the march was supposed to start at half past but there were only a few dozen people standing around. We examined them closely from the safety of the pine trees. What exactly did a commie look like? Or even more interestingly, a lesbo? Mostly the people milling around were in their twenties, university types. There were a lot of natural wool jerseys on show but apart from that they appeared pretty normal. In the absence of any obvious distinguishing features we agreed that maybe all the women there were lesbians.

For all the Templeton girls' talk they hadn't put in an appearance. Mrs Montgomery was there, though. She'd had the march poster up in her front window for weeks. And there were others. For some reason old Mr Robinson who'd come to the beach that day with his rope, hoping to help a stranded whale, was there. It was a surprise to see him wearing clothes other than his togs and without a towel hung around his neck. There were a number of older sisters of boys that we knew, girls who had gone off to t-coll or to do nursing. There was also a teacher from school, Mr

Jenson. He was only in his second year of teaching and we were aware that he wasn't that much older than the seventh formers. Still, young or not, we were surprised to see a teacher taking part in such an anti-social gathering.

By six forty the crowd had grown to about fifty. The woman in the purple dress stood up on the box and welcomed everyone. She had long black hair tied back in a pony-tail, and the narrow face of a pixie. She kept on glancing toward the edges of the park as though expecting a sudden throng to appear, bursting through the bushes. But no one else showed and eventually she introduced the main speaker as the leader of the southern branch of Halt All Racist Tours. The man from HART had apparently been to South Africa and had met with the leaders of the anti-apartheid movement there at considerable risk to himself. We anticipated a burly figure but when he got up to speak he was small and fragile looking and spoke in a gentle voice. He stood too far back from the microphone. The thin crowd shuffled forward, people cocking their heads to the side to hear, like brown sparrows clustering over a handful of crumbs.

Back near the trees we could not hear anything he said. His speech was entirely lost among the whish of the easterly wind in the branches above us. There was a roar of revved engine and a burst of throbbing music. It was an orange Datsun that sounded as if it had a hole in the exhaust pipe. We vaguely recognised the driver as a guy from up North Brighton. He was nineteen or twenty and a friend of Brent Cox. There was another guy next to him in the passenger seat and at least three more in the back. The driver accelerated the car as he passed the park, gunning the engine and blasting on the horn. There were a few shouts and then the car sped off into the night. The HART guy kept on speaking.

Any thought that the interruption was coincidental vanished when the Datsun returned a couple of minutes later. The tyres squealed beyond the low bushes and there was a puff of white smoke. There was shouting and laughter. The guy from HART still kept on talking but a lot of people in the crowd turned and looked towards the road and we could see them shaking their heads.

The speaker was not dynamic enough to whip up any obvious enthusiasm from the small crowd. Perhaps sensing that he was losing his audience, he finally announced that the march would begin. A banner was unfurled and the woman in the purple dress took one pole and the speaker the other. It had grown dark while the speeches were going on, in the slow, almost imperceptible way that night seeps into open spaces. When the banner was raised it was hard for us to read what was written on it. Others raised smaller banners and home-made placards. People switched on torches and the march set off out of the park and on to Marine Parade where they swung towards the shopping centre.

To us the whole thing looked pretty ridiculous. Fifty or so people walking slowly behind a banner in the gloom wasn't our idea of a real protest. It was not the raging revolt we had imagined. It was more like a Plunket group out for a stroll. As if sensing that something was missing (five hundred or so more people, perhaps) the woman in the purple dress produced a megaphone. We trailed behind on our bikes and listened to her broadcast slogans into the darkness. She spoke in a hollow voice about the Springbok tour as a sign that New Zealand supported apartheid. 'Stop the tour!' she intoned. She quoted figures about the number of blacks killed by the South African police every year. 'Stop the tour!' A lot of it we only half understood. Some of it we simply didn't believe. 'Stop the tour' she implored the pulled curtains and closed doors of the houses she passed.

The group marched on, in and out of the street-lights, their torches bobbing along in the thickening dark. The voice of the woman with the megaphone called for the people inside their homes to come out and join them. She harangued the front fences and hedges, the white trellises and concrete flamingos. She told them that they had 'nothing to fear, but fear itself' (even we recognised that by using that one she was plagiarising material from another, more popular, movement).

The marchers seemed to be warming up, though. Stop the tour! became a louder chant. Nearly everyone joined in when the woman called for a song. 'We Shall

Overcome' rose up, surprisingly beautiful. By the time they approached the Empire the group were well into the second rendition.

All the noise drew the men drinking in the Empire out on to the street. They spilled out of the big front doors, some of them swaying slightly, others with sloppy grins painted on their faces. Their happy beer buzz was blown into tatters when they saw the marchers. They took in the banners and the driptailed signs and instinctively knew that they didn't like what they were seeing. In the pale street-light the men could read enough to know that they were being attacked on some fundamental level.

NEW ZEALANDERS UNITED AGAINST APARTHEID

The main banner was a bit wordy and it probably took the half-cut regulars outside the Empire a few rereadings to fully come to terms with it, but the sentiment was plain enough. One marcher was holding a square of white cardboard nailed to a tomato stake. On it was painted, WE DON'T WANT YOUR RACIST TOUR. Another read, RUGBY=RACISM. That particular message was pretty easy to understand and would've gone down like a truck full of wet pig-shit with the blokes at the Empire. We didn't think much of it ourselves.

Tug Gardiner and Jase Harbidge had ridden up past the marchers. They were on the other side of the road from the pub, their feet on the footpath, but they were still sitting on the seats of their bikes. They said later that they could hear the angry growl of the men. Tug said it was a low rumble, like the workings of some old half-forgotten machine as it slowly started up.

'Who do they think ... stirrers ... bloody commies coming down here ... my dad died in the war ... poofters... lefties ... decent family men who've played ... still love the game ... only a game ... rugby is rugby and politics is something else ... who the hell do they think they are, calling *me* racist? ... bullshit-bloodybullshit ... fuckin dykes and commies stirring things up when they don't have to. Finger pointers. No hopers! Wankers!'

The machine rumbled up through the gears.

The marchers didn't seem to be anticipating any real trouble. We saw the danger long before they did. They were on the footpath on the same side of the road as the Empire and still singing. The pixie-faced woman in the purple dress and the guy from HART were out front still holding the banner. The others followed close behind, four or five abreast, the middle of the march bulging slightly so that some people spilled on to the road.

When they were almost at the hotel the front of the protest met a wall of angry men. All signs of joviality had gone from the faces of the Empire's pa-trons. They wore granite masks and stood with their arms folded across their chests. The singing faded and the group shuffled to a halt. Without seeming to confer, the line of mostly women at the front of the march moved sideways, off the footpath and on to the road. Silently they skirted the men. No one moved to stop them but the men's dark muttering grew in volume. It turned into sporadic shouts and then jeering. 'We Want Rugby!' Someone yelled. 'We Want Rugby!' Other men picked up the cry and soon it was an openmouthed beery broadside into the passing column of marchers.

A few of the anti-tour protesters, mostly people on the edge of the group, began to return the shouts. There were angry faces on both sides now. But most of the marchers put their heads down, averting their eyes from the wall of men. They moved quickly, clearly intimidated by the glowering, shouting crowd. A few of the younger ones stopped, though they risked getting left behind by the bulk of the march as it flowed around them.

The ones who stopped, no more than half a dozen, faced off against the pro-tour crowd. Only a few metres separated the two groups. There were twenty-five or so from the Empire and they were physically bigger and more intimidating. We knew who we had our money on if things turned nasty. Tiny Wilson was there and he still played lock for the local club's masters team. Mr Bonniston, the butcher, was in the thick of things too. He was no soft-cock.

The woman in the purple dress was now holding the megaphone at her side and she also stopped to address the men. We didn't hear what she said but there were jeers. She seemed to be speaking to the five or six men directly in front of her. Some dag loudly called out something about dykes and fingers. We heard that clear enough. All the men laughed.

'Piss off home, love. You're not welcome here.' We heard that too.

The guy from HART joined her. He also began to talk to the crowd. There were louder shouts. A guy was a better target than a woman. Within seconds the whole front row was yelling at him. A big guy, six foot with a beer gut hanging over his belt, stepped forward and shoved the HART guy in the chest. He staggered backwards but was caught by the marchers behind him and did not fall. More of the protesters stopped moving forwards. They turned and squared off against the group on the footpath.

The Empire has a long balcony on the street side leading off the upstairs rooms. Something heavy and white thudded to the ground right in the middle of the protest group. There were several screams and the woman in purple dropped the megaphone.

A white cloud enveloped them. For a moment it looked as though a freak weather pattern had brought down a patch of fog over the marchers. Flour. We realised that some joker had thrown a full bag of flour from the balcony. The bag must have been partly open because the contents had spilled out even before it hit the ground. We watched the cloud settle gently on the marchers' clothes and on their hair. They became photo negatives of themselves against the darkness. We looked up and saw that there were about four or five guys up on the balcony. They began to throw other things. Small missiles flew through the air, hit the road and shattered. Now it was eggs. One hit a protester on the shoulder and yolk splattered up over her cheek. She screamed.

The men on the footpath were laughing. One of the marchers on the edge of the crowd had had enough. He shoved a guy who was still shouting abuse. We saw that it was Mr Jenson, the teacher from school, who was doing the shoving. The guy shoved him back and then they had each other by the shirt fronts. The two crowds merged around them and a couple of punches were thrown. Surprisingly (to us), it was the heckler and not the young English teacher who staggered back clutching his face. Men from both groups rushed to join in and we lost sight of Mr Jenson in the flurry of flailing arms and short vicious jabs.

People from both groups jumped in to join the fight or to try and break apart the fighters. Old Mr Robinson was in there, trying to restrain a drinker twice his size. We saw that Robinson was in danger of getting clocked himself. There was Jenson again, fiery eyed, nose to nose with an equally worked-up rugby supporter. They were yelling into each other's faces.

'Racist!

'Traitor!'

'You're pig ignorant, mate!'

'Go back to Russia, you communist!'

They were both still yelling abuse when they were pulled apart. Other people from both groups were dragged back into the ranks.

For lack of any real alternative the march carried on. The pixie-faced woman with the megaphone was silent, staring straight ahead. There was flour on her hair and egg on her dress. All of the protesters looked grim and several of the younger women were crying. What the organisers must have hoped would be a show of solidarity and strength against the Springbok tour now resembled nothing more than a straggling group of refugees. Several of the men had cuts and bruises on their faces. Others limped as they brushed at the flour on their clothes. Everyone seemed to be in shock but they marched on stoically. The two holding the main banner were almost side by side so that the words sagged and were unreadable. There was no more singing. The torches were all on now and as we trailed further behind, the body of the march looked like a lit ship, damaged and listing, slipping away into the darkness to sink.

Luckily only a few of the men from the Empire bothered to follow. The ones who felt the most aggrieved shadowed the march for a while, taunting and jeering, 'We Want Rugby!' until, getting no response, they too turned and drifted back to the Empire. No doubt they stood around the bar until closing time and recounted the role each had played, with the vigour associated with fishing stories or old rugby games.

Some of the marchers began to drop out. People simply moved to the side without comment, singly and in pairs, so that the march moved away from them. Enough was enough. They could tell people that they'd done their bit. No doubt they would use the side streets to avoid the Empire on the way back to their cars.

The march was supposed to finish at the mall, where there were going to be more speeches. But when the group finally arrived at the space outside Farmers, the woman in the purple dress and a few other organisers huddled together. There was very little lighting in the mall. The roar of a cruising car could still occasionally be heard in the distance. We sat on our bikes back in the shadows and watched as the woman in purple said a few words. Maybe the megaphone had been broken when she dropped it outside the Empire, because now she spoke without it. Mind you, the group was so small by that point she hardly need to be amplified. Only about twenty people stood in front of her. The remaining marchers shone their torches in the speaker's direction so that she had twenty shadows scattered around her. When she finished speaking, the people who were left quickly dispersed and went home.

We were biking back down Rocking Horse Road when Mark Murray said, 'Mr Jenson's first name is Simon.' In the end it was as simple as that.

We tried to discover all that we could about SJ. We quickly found out that he was twenty-three years old and unmarried. He had moved north from Dunedin at the beginning of '81 and his voice carried a hint of southern burr; the Rs in the words 'Shakespeare' and 'pentameter' rolled like a sea-swell into the end of his sentences. SJ rented a two-bedroom cottage near the middle of Rocking Horse Road, only five minutes' walk down from the Ashers' dairy. It was an old bach, barely more than four rooms and a corrugated-iron roof, with the edges of the garden plots marked by hundreds of whitewashed rocks the size of fists. The bach sat in the middle of a quarter-acre section, the back of which was only distinguishable from the dunes by two strands of sagging wire.

Enquiry revealed that SJ was well liked by his students, the girls at least. They considered him handsome. We felt uncomfortable about judging his physical attractiveness. SJ was tallish. His eyes were brown. His hair was dark and slightly longer than was normal for a teacher. But we were reluctant to draw any conclusions from the parts of the man we could observe. Only Matt Templeton with his five older sisters was unequivocal in his assessment: 'Sure, girls would go ga-ga over him.'

Between the girls in SJ's classes, petty rivalries and jealousies darted like lightning. Not that SJ seemed to do anything to feed the girls' interest. Nor did he show favour. Even Martha Ferguson, the plainest of the plain, had occasionally been given a smile and an encouraging word. Martha was a member of the photography club that SJ ran after school every Wednesday. All but one of the members were girls, and the only boy had an undisguised interest in theatre: he was a sixth former regularly referred to as 'the poofter'. Most boys who had been taught by SJ simply reported him to be an okay teacher.

In our interview with Martha, she described SJ as being 'different' since the new school year had begun. 'In what way?' we asked, anticipating a revelation. Her plain, round face gazed earnestly up at us and her mouth gaped like a deep-sea fish in a rock pool. 'It's like,' she said at last, and sighed deeply, 'like he's gone away and now all that's left is his body.'

At every opportunity we trailed through the school behind SJ, down the corridors and over the parched school grounds, like blowflies behind a shit-stained dog. Our eyes crawled all over him.

June rolled over into July and with real winter came the first disharmony in our ranks. The afternoon meetings in Jim Turner's garage became tense as we debated what to do next. SJ had done nothing incriminating, or even unpredictable, for three weeks. Apart from his damning initials, and a plain girl's opinion that he was 'different', we had nothing. One faction, led by Roy Moynahan, wanted to make an anonymous call to the police telling them of SJ's identity. There was a special phone number still occasionally being advertised in the paper for people with information about Lucy's murder. It must also be said that Roy and Al Penny and a couple of others had wanted to hand the diary over right away but had been outvoted.

Jase Harbidge was the most vocal against both ideas. Jase argued the best we could count on from the police was that they would interview SJ. 'If he's covered his tracks and he's a good liar he'll walk away, no worries. It happens all the time.'

Our arguments went nowhere. We were like two tug-of-war team so evenly matched that neither side moves an inch.

It came as a surprise when Jase and Pete Marshall took it upon themselves to end the statement by breaking into SJ's house. It was not a group decision. They arranged to meet near his place at a time they knew SJ would be teaching his fourth form English class. It was a Friday, July the sixth, and a few dark clouds were hanging around out to sea—a big southerly storm was predicted for that evening.

Pete told us later that they left their bikes in the overgrown section next door to SJ's rented house. They stood in the long grass gathering up their courage. The grass was wet from an earlier light rain and it shivered and shook itself dry in the cold easterly.

Pete and Jase entered SJ's section where broken boards in the fence had left a gap. They came out behind the garden shed with its two-stroke mower visible through the open door. The back of the house was locked but Jase broke the lower pane of glass with an old rugby sock that he'd found hanging on the line and wrapped around one of the whitewashed stones from the garden. He reached through gingerly and flicked a latch. Suddenly, against all their expectations, they were in.

Pete told some of us privately that Jase immediately began to pull drawers out and empty the contents on to the lino. 'He seemed really mad. He just went nuts. I didn't think it was a good idea to try and stop him.' Knives and forks and spoons monsooned down, along with whisks and corkscrews and an eggbeater. Soon the kitchen floor was flooded with cutlery.

Jase and Pete did not know what they were looking for and Pete admitted that very soon it didn't matter. In a later interview, he confessed to personally hurling a bag of flour against the kitchen wall so that it exploded in a white cloud. All the food was pulled from the cupboards. Packets lay scattered around. Dried macaroni and cornflakes crackled beneath their shoes like shells in the silvery water. Eggs were thrown against the walls. The hot tap was left running, in imitation of the anti-tour protest.

When they were finished in the kitchen they moved on. SJ's bedroom was quickly turned upside down. His surprisingly small collection of clothes was tossed around the room and a couple of shirts ended up ripped. The sheets on his bed were roughly stripped off and the mattress tipped from the wire base so that it lay drunkenly, half blocking the door.

The second bedroom had been converted into a darkroom. When they opened that door a heady aroma of chemicals poured out. Pete fumbled along the wall for the light switch. When he finally found it, they saw that the windows were blacked out with sheets of black polythene, taped down at the edges. A trestle-table against the wall was covered with plastic bottles of developer and fixer. SJ even had an enlarger, tall and spidery, where images could be manipulated. The packet of photographs was sitting in plain view. It was Jase who picked it up and slipped out the prints. Jase has always been reluctant to talk about what happened that morning, possibly because of guilt about what he did to SJ's home. Maybe he still feels a lingering outrage at what he discovered there. But years later Pete still remembered hearing Jase gasp as though he had been sucker-punched in the stomach.

Even by today's standards the pictures of Lucy were pornographic.

Southerly storms were not unusual on the east coast. Every winter they blew up from Antarctica, blustery and laced with froth from the Southern Ocean. It was the intensity of the storm that hit on July 6 1981 that caught everyone off guard. Of course there are no hard and fast rules when it comes to the weather. People forget that the *Wahine* was sunk in '68 by a storm that came out of nowhere. That was the roof-lifter that our parents spoke about with awe.

By mid-afternoon the wind had risen to a howl. Although no one was down on the beach to see it, we could all hear the waves thrashing the shore. Although it wasn't raining yet, the temperature had dropped sharply. After school we walked and pedalled down the road with debris from knocked-over rubbish-bins blowing around us and sand plucked from the dunes stinging any exposed skin. We arrived in the Turners' garage raw. The photographs awaited us, fanned out on the pool table. The wind pushed through the cracks in the walls and fingered their edges. It stirred the dry piles of spilled sheep-shit in the corner and buffeted the yellowed clippings pinned to the walls so that they rustled uneasily.

It is not an exaggeration to say that we were appalled by the photos. Our faith was shaken. We could not match the Lucy we knew with this brazen doppelgänger spread out in front of us.

The pictures were obviously taken on several different occasions. In some, Lucy's hair was tied back with a ribbon. In others she wore unbecoming make-up. Our Lucy pouted and posed like a stranger. Most of us had seen her naked before, on the beach, in the half-hour before the forensics people screened her off, but we had subsequently convinced ourselves that it was the type of nudity we associated with children, with sisters and mothers. There was an innocence to Lucy in death that these photographs called a lie. Our treasured memories of her were defiled in front of us.

There was absolutely no doubt in our minds that SJ had murdered Lucy. We agreed that she must have seen the huge mistake she was making by involving herself with someone capable of twisting her in this way. We quickly saw how things must have gone. After he somehow duped her into posing for these photographs, Lucy must have tried to call it off. In a fit of rage he had strangled her. It was obvious. Wasn't it also likely (more than likely, probable) that he had manipulated her (blackmailed her) into posing for these photographs in the first place? Of course it was. What other explanation could there be?

When we couldn't stand them any more, Jase Harbidge gathered all the photographs together. There was no question of taking them to the police, even though we knew they were important evidence. It was bad enough that we had seen them. We're not ashamed to say that more than one of us was openly upset as Jase carried the photographs outside. We stood in the lee of the garage, beneath the last autumn leaves still stubbornly clinging to the pear tree. The Turners had a rusting, half-gallon drum that Jim's dad used for his bonfires. The drum had a lid, and inside, it was half full of leaves and twigs that were still dry. We all watched in silence as Jase tipped the photographs inside the drum. Roy Moynahan had a box of matches in his pocket along with his Marlboros. The wind blew out several matches before we clustered around in a circle tight enough to create some shelter. The dry leaves caught first and then the photographs. They curled up from the outside in. The chemicals made the flames flare orange and yellow.

Even on the far side of the garage, the southerly sought us out. It swirled and eddied, snatching at the burning contents of the drum. No one had thought to put the lid back on, and flaming leaves and half photos rose up past us into the air. They were tossed wherever the wind saw fit. Some blew into our faces, causing us to scatter and swat at our heads as though we were under attack from a nest of wasps. Flaming photographs caught in the branches of the pear tree. More went up and over the roof of the Turners' house. Several blew sideways across the lawn at ground level and then caught in the hedge.

A few months before, when the drought was at its worst, we would have set fire to the garage and the house and probably to the whole Spit. Even with the recent rain, the hedge was still dry at its centre. Several small fires caught and flared up inside it. We stamped and beat them into submission the best we could but there were more flare-ups and some threatened to grow out of control. Jim eventually thought to get his father's garden hose.

By the time we had put out the hedge fires and checked that there were no other fires around the Turners' house, the photographs were gone. Either they had been consumed, rendered down into single layers of ash or, more likely, they had blown away into the night. We imagined them flaming upwards.

Al Penny, quite recently, recalled a fleeting second where he had looked up into the low dark sky and, through the branches of the pear tree, had seen Lucy's face, cleansed by the flames, as she smiled down at him. 'She was so beautiful. And then she was gone.'

Later we went back to our homes and had dinner with our families as though nothing were wrong. If we were more surly or distracted than usual, no one bothered to comment. Our families were used to our secrets and our sullen silences, which by then they mostly labelled 'teenage moods' and shrugged off.

The storm proper hit as most of us were eating our dinners. The wind suddenly began to blow even harder. The rain flung itself at our homes, rattling the glass in the windows, beating on our roofs with wet fists. Everyone had to raise their voices to be heard. After dinner, the televisions were turned up until they blared. The late news led with the damage the storm had caused in Dunedin and in the other cities and towns further south than us. Roofs had been lifted, cars turned over on exposed stretches of road. There was heavy flooding nearly everywhere. Stormwater systems could not cope with the record rainfalls. Wry shopkeepers were shown wading down aisles, moving stock on to higher shelves. One old bloke, still in his pyjamas, gave the thumbs up as he was carried by a fireman from a flooded rest home. The highway south of Timaru was closed because the ocean had sent waves big enough to undermine a stretch of road, which had crumbled into the sea.

But we did not need the television to tell us about the force of the storm. We watched the way our fathers tensed with each unfamiliar noise from outside; listening for the crack of falling branches, or the scream of nails pulling free. Our mothers were either silent and serious as they served up our meals, or they put on masks of jovial good humour. Which was more painful was hard to say.

Tug Gardiner woke in the night. He lay listening to the rain, which was still throwing itself against the roof and walls of his raised room. The room now felt to him like a boat trying to ride out the storm. The red numbers on his alarm-radio glowed 12:30. He'd been woken by a dream. It had been about Lucy. The dream had snapped him into consciousness like a slap. He was wide awake and his pyjamas were soaked with sweat, though it was cold in his room.

'I knew for sure I had to go,' he told us later. He dressed in the dark and climbed down the steep steps from his room as quietly as he could manage. His raincoat was in the hall cupboard, where he also found his father's golf bag. Tug pulled a wedge free and felt its weight. He swung it experimentally in the narrow hall and then, satisfied, he let himself out into the night.

At houses up and down Rocking Horse Road we were doing the same. Each of us had woken at the same time as Tug, 12:30. We woke sure of what we had to do. We are the first to admit that the whole idea is ridiculous when committed to paper. Here on the page, in black and white, it is absurd—something we would normally dismiss as the worst sort of nonsense. But the truth is that the dream was exactly the same for each of us. We *all* dreamt of Lucy that night. She was standing on the beach at the spot where Pete Marshall had found her body. She was clothed in a soft white light and there was a small finger-bone of driftwood in her matted hair. We could see the circling bruises around her neck. Lucy's eyes were fixed on ours. She did not speak but wore an expression of unfathomable sadness. She implored us. Even without words we knew what she was asking.

Only Jase Harbidge encountered any difficulty in getting away. When Jase passed, fully dressed, through his darkened kitchen on his way to the back door, he found his father sitting at the kitchen table staring at one of his wedding photographs by the light from the hall, where the bulb was always left burning. Bill Harbidge took in the heavy crowbar that hung from Jase's hand.

'I've gotta go out,' said Jase.

'Sure,' his dad said and glanced towards the window where the rain dripped down the glass. He went to the fridge and began making himself a sandwich. Jase watched him but was unsure of what else to say, so he just turned and walked out of the house.

The wind seemed to have lessened slightly but the rain was still falling when we slipped from our homes. Like the stormwater systems down south, the gutters and underground pipes down New Brighton could not cope with so much water in such a short period of time. Rocking Horse Road had started to flood hours before and large pools of rainwater were now lapping against the edges of the footpaths. In some places the water from both sides of the road had met in the middle, forming dark lakes through which we waded.

Tug met Pete Marshall near the Ashers' dairy. As though their meeting had been planned, they fell into step, although neither of them spoke. Jim Turner reported seeing Jase ahead of him on the road. Others were drawn to the beach and the light from their torches flickered and wove down through the sand dunes as they followed the tracks. Behind the dunes, foaming white waves stampeded on to the beach.

We converged on SJ's house, coming out of the surrounding darkness singly and in pairs. Tug and Pete were the first to arrive. Tug's hood was back up. He tapped the head of his golf club with a metallic watch-tick against a fencepost as he waited. Jim Turner had blacked his face with shoe polish so that the whites of his eyes showed bright in what little light there was. Both Al Penny and Matt Templeton wore balaclavas and Mark Murray carried a softball bat. Pete Marshall had stopped to collect Lucy's trophy from the Turners' garage and bore it through the night like a silver talisman. No one mentioned the dream.

When we had all gathered on the street, we walked on to SJ's front lawn. For a moment we were at a loss. The dream had brought us here but had not told us what to do when we arrived. The only light came from a naked bulb above the front door. We were facing south and the rain drove into us; those who weren't already saturated, soon were.

Although we did not notice it straight away, the rain had already formed puddles on the lawn where the ground was low-lying. One puddle was reaching out to embrace another and another. If we'd cared to look we would have seen the same thing happening in front of all the houses we had passed. The road flooding was not unprecedented, but elsewhere on the Spit puddles were unnatural. Water normally vanished instantly into the sand. But we were not interested in the puddles or even in the storm. Our focus was on the house.

Mild Al Penny was the first to throw one of the whitewashed rocks that ringed the garden. The rock arced through the darkness. We watched its progress as it travelled through the air and then carried on through the bedroom window. The shatter of glass cut through the noise of the wind and the rain. There was a pause, and then the bedroom lit up. We could all see SJ clearly as he peered out through the ragged pane. He had been startled from sleep and was wide-eyed. As more rocks began to hit the house, his head darted back inside and the light in the bedroom was turned off.

There were more than enough rocks, hundreds. Some bounced off the weatherboards, others found their mark. More glass shattered and fell and not just in the bedroom either. The windows of the darkroom and the lounge and the louvred panes in the toilet all shattered. The rocks that went high landed on the iron roof. They roared and growled as they rolled back down, adding their voices to the storm's.

And then SJ was standing on his front step. He had pulled on a T-shirt but was still wearing his pyjama pants. He was lit from above so that we could not see his eyes. Where they should have been there were only dark sea-caves inside which, we were certain, lurked a black soul. He shouted garbled, angry threats into the darkness but he might as well have been yelling at the slanting rain. We knew that he could not see us, or if he could, that we were only darker shadows in the night.

Who threw that next rock? We don't know (even if we did, we wouldn't tell, right to this day). All that we will say is that it was a good throw, hard and accurate. The rock struck SJ on the forehead just above his left eyebrow. A communal sigh of satisfaction rose from us. There was immediately blood and SJ clutched at his head and staggered forward. That involuntary movement took him down the single concrete step, out of the light from the bulb above the door. Perhaps if we had been able to see him more clearly, what happened next would have been avoided. Then again, probably not.

More white rocks flew, striking him on the body. Nobody was holding back now and we were not kids any more. At fifteen the power in your arm is there and your eyesight is sharp. SJ staggered again and fell. He tried to regain his feet. White rocks flew in like tracer in the night. Behind the dunes the waves crashed. The storm rumbled above and the wind howled. The rain beat down on us and him. We closed in, forming a wide semi-circle in the darkness. A large rock struck his left knee and he cried out and fell again. He did not try to get up this time but simply curled up in a ball and took all that we had to give. By then he had stopped shouting, and if SJ was moaning we could not hear it above the rushing sound in our ears.

When the rocks close to us finally ran out we threw whatever was at hand. The golf club helicoptered through the air into his body. Someone threw a potted geranium that fell short, the pot shattering. In the end we resorted to snatching up the very earth. We hurled the sodden sand, darting forward, yelling in berserk, open-mouthed rage. The silver trophy was the last to go. It pierced the darkness, striking SJ on the shoulder where he lay, still now. The silver girl broke as she rebounded, the metal separating from the plinth where it was only glued, and both parts lay on the ground.

We had glimpses of each other's faces but quickly looked away. Something primitive and savage was there: a look we has also seen in the faces of the men who confronted the protesters outside the Empire.

The Molotov cocktail was improvised on the spot (though again, who did it, we cannot say). A tin of two-stroke petrol, intended for the lawnmower, had been taken from the unlocked garden shed, along with an old rag. A glass-milk bottle from next to the letterbox. Once assembled the cocktail would have welcomed a flame as a natural progression. It flew through the air and into the bedroom. There was a pause and then a pleasing whoosh. The fire spread quickly. The black polythene covering the darkroom window melted away, curling in on itself, and the long flames tasted the outside air. Despite the rain the fire quickly reached out and up into the roof, and then the flames were flickering through the broken glass of the other bedroom as well. Flames stalked the house, moving quickly from room to room. We soon felt the heat on our faces, even though our backs were chilled and stiff. In no time, the flames had a stranglehold on the house. We had to move back or risk being scorched.

We stood, panting from the exertion, watching the raging fire. Our anger had been building up since Jase had found the photographs of Lucy. In fact, it's probable that it had been building since Pete had discovered her body on the beach. Now at last it was exorcised. Nobody spoke or met anyone else's eye.

Only now did we notice that the lawn was completely flooded. Where we had scooped sand was under water. Water lapped at our ankles. Looking around we saw that the road and the sections of the nearby houses were all the same.

We didn't know what to do or what to think so we just stood, ankle deep, watching the fire. We stood like that for what seemed a long time. The firelight reflected in the surface of the water. We ignored SJ. He lay on his back, still, light and dark flickering across him. He was no more to us now than a bag of old clothes someone had discarded in the rising water. It was only when the first siren sounded, still far away, thin and whiny like a mosquito in the night, that we were roused from our trance. One by one we turned and walked away into the darkness of Rocking Horse Road.

The nay-sayers' worst predictions about the Spit had finally come true. On the night of July 6, 1981, the Spit sank beneath the waves.

What had happened was that the huge downpour, two hundred millimetres in less than eight hours, had combined with an unusually high tide. The rain had sunk down into the sand of the Spit as it usually did, but had met the elevated water-table, until finally the water had had nowhere left to go.

All up and down the Spit, people and animals became confused as to where the ocean and the estuary started and finished. As he walked home in the darkness Jim Turner saw a school of silver herring swimming down the middle of Rocking Horse Road. The light from his torch flashed off their sides and they darted left and right, away from the bow wave Jim's feet pushed in front of him. Roy Moynahan told us of being almost home and standing on a small stingray that twisted and turned under his foot so that he fell. Later he found the razor cut in his jeans where its tail had slashed. We agreed that he was lucky not to have been badly cut. For weeks afterwards people living down the Spit spoke of finding dried starfish in gutters and gardens. Hardy crabs turned up still alive under woodpiles and in drains months later. There was even a story going around that someone sat on their outdoor toilet and felt something tickle their bum. When he or she (it varies in the telling) jumped up and peered into the bowl they found a fair-sized octopus curled up down there.

Standing in the driveway of his parents' house Tug Gardiner looked across the flooded road and saw the Ashers. They were on the front step of the dairy. The light was on in the shop so he could see them clearly. It was the first time we could remember seeing all three of them together since Lucy's funeral. Even though it was the middle of the night they were all fully dressed. Tug told us that they did not speak but just stood and looked out at the water, which had risen up past the second step and was moments away from spilling over into the shop. He watched them for a long time, and even after the water rose up and touched their feet they did not move. 'It was impossible to tell what they were thinking,' said Tug.

When dawn came, it revealed an almost continuous stretch of water right through from the estuary to the sand dunes. Apart from the dunes and the rectangular roofs of the houses, the Spit had sunk back into the ocean. That was the photo on the front page of *The Press* the following day; an aerial shot, taken from a helicopter, in which you could see the roofs of nearly all of our homes (The Press, *July 7. Exhibit 124).*

The flood waters only rose until the rain stopped and the tide fell, which was just before dawn. Then the flooding started to vanish as quickly as it had appeared. By mid-morning the water had already soaked down into the sand. All that was left was the damage. In our homes the carpets were sodden and smelt of the sea, and of the estuary. A ring of wet sand was left around the walls just above the skirting. By lunchtime our fathers had began to call their insurance companies and by evening assessors were roaming our homes. Men in suits opened silted ovens and peered into our wardrobes where our shoes lay draped in seaweed.

Our fathers took time off work. They spent the next week ripping up carpets and throwing ruined furniture into piles. We helped haul sodden wool and rubber underlay out into communal skips that appeared on the road. Our mothers mostly remained inside, grimly scrubbing at the walls and vacuuming bare floorboards until we couldn't stand the noise.

Eventually the insurance companies paid out and we ended up helping repaint all the rooms. We helped haul in new couches and televisions. We watched men staple new carpet over the boards. With all the changes, we began to feel that we were living in different homes from the ones we had grown up in.

There were different smells, the musk of new carpet and that sharp chemistry of fresh paint. There were unfamiliar colours everywhere.

The Springboks slipped into the country on July 19. We were too busy with the clean-up and coping with all the changes to get excited by their arrival.

Even the beach was different after the storm. Cliffs of sand rose up where once there had been gently sloping dunes. Several of the landmark pines down in the reserve had been blown over, and within weeks they were cut up with chainsaws and the wood hauled away by men with hungry fireplaces and an eye for a bargain. Jim Turner's father told the insurance man that the flooding had done considerable damage to his garage. One whole wall apparently collapsed in the storm. We all suspected that Mr Turner's own efforts with a rope tied to the back of his neighbour's car had a lot more to do with the damage than the southerly. When Al recovered all our stuff from the garage the morning after the storm all four walls were still standing. Either way, the garage was demolished and replaced with a new aluminium one, paid for by the insurance company. The pool table was hauled off to the dump, and although Jim's dad said he would replace it, he never got around to finding another one.

Our world had also changed in more subtle ways. We now had to take our shoes off at the doors of our homes, and hose down our feet when we came inside from the beach. Items of furniture that had been damaged by the water were replaced and our mothers also seized the opportunity to rearrange the old stuff. We now bashed our shins in our own homes when we attempted to navigate our way in the darkness. Some of us found ourselves sleeping on new beds, in rooms where our rugby posters and advertising for the tour were not allowed to be pinned back up for the sake of the new paint. A lot of our personal stuff had been damaged by the water; anything that had been below knee height. Clothing, shoes and favourite tapes, ghetto blasters and old school projects had all been chucked on to the skips.

At first the undamaged stuff was tidied away in cupboards, but then when it became apparent that life had moved on, it was put into plastic rubbish bags and left out on the footpath to be taken away. The upshot of it all was that after the flood of '81, which was what everyone began calling it, we started to feel like strangers in our own homes. We awoke in the night and didn't know where we were.

Our thoughts turned to the lives we would have when we inevitably broke from our parents and struck out by ourselves in the world. For the first time in our lives, that seemed like a real possibility.

SEVEN

For the record, we did not kill SJ. He suffered a severe concussion and needed twenty-three stitches to his head *(Medical Report. Exhibit 88).* His left wrist was broken, probably by the impact of the golf club. His left knee was shattered and had to be reconstructed and, the doctor's report noted, later in life he would probably suffer from rheumatism in that joint. We are not sure if that prophecy has come to pass. SJ also had extensive bruising to his back and legs, which had taken the brunt of the stones.

All up, he spent ten days in hospital, during which the police interviewed him twice. The first time was in regard to the attack on him. Against our expectations SJ must have recognised at least one of us, because the police moved quickly. We were all picked up in the days following the storm and were questioned separately and made to give formal statements. We tried to explain to the interviewing officers how we had come to know Lucy Asher, what she meant to us. From their blank looks, it was plain that they didn't get it. In the end we gave up and just stuck to the basic facts, to yes and no answers. We won't deny that we were scared, but the truth was that after the police heard what we had to say about Lucy's diary and the photographs, their focus quickly shifted. We had offered them a bigger fish to fry.

During their second interview with SJ the police wanted to talk to him exclusively about the murder of Lucy Asher. They quickly established two things. Firstly that he had been sleeping with Lucy. And secondly that, during the weekend Lucy had been killed, SJ was staying with his parents in Dunedin. He had been best man at his older brother's wedding. More than sixty witnesses could vouch for him on the night Lucy was murdered.

The truth came out as easily as that. SJ had not murdered Lucy Asher, after all. He had committed no crime, not in a strictly legal sense. Lucy had been of age. SJ was guilty only of an indiscretion and a betrayal of the school's trust. He declined to press charges against the 'unidentified youths' who had assaulted him *(The Press, July 9, 1981. Exhibit 125)*, undoubtedly out of fear of what would be reported in the papers about him if the case went to trial. It was a course of action we're sure the police strongly advised him to follow. Jase Harbidge's dad was still a cop and had influence. Each of us got off with a strong lecture from the police on the dangers of 'vigilante justice', and we were passed back into the care of our parents. They were, in most cases, less understanding than the police had been and more drawn out with their punishments. Several of us were forbidden to go to the Springbok game at Lancaster Park. That was a bitter blow.

The day he got out of hospital SJ packed his car with what little he could salvage from the gutted shell of the house, and left South Brighton High School and the Spit forever. None of us was there to see him leave. We do know that he moved to Australia about six months later, where he taught for a while but then gave teaching away. We last followed up on SJ a few years ago: he was married with twin sons, then in their teens, and living in Adelaide, where he worked for Fuji Xerox as some type of middle manager.

Pete Marshall died on October 31 last year, only four months after he was diagnosed with cancer. He was forty-one, the same age as the rest of us. Pete left instructions that he wanted his funeral service to be held outside. 'I want it under the sky. I don't want any fucking roof,' is what he told us from his final bed. We passed on the sentiment, if not the exact wording, to the Anglican minister who delivered the service. A nice guy, even if he was a little bit overeager. Grant Webb referred to him as 'the Labrador', and we knew what he meant. The guy was all barely restrained enthusiasm and bouncing good humour.

The funeral was held on the lawn out the back of the crematorium on Linwood Ave. It is close enough to the estuary for you to smell the mud at low tide. The place has a smallish lawn surrounded by a low hedge and beds of white roses, which were long before their best on the day. Spring weather is unpredictable and we were lucky it didn't rain. The wind was cold and small white clouds skimmed over the sky. People came rugged up. There weren't that many mourners, not as many as you'd expect for a guy as likeable as Pete. The funeral director obviously hadn't known how many were going to come, and we hadn't been able to tell him, so he'd put out too many of those folding wooden chairs. It was a pity because the empty chairs on the lawn made the group look even smaller, as if a lot of people hadn't bothered to show up.

Pete's father had died ten years earlier and his mother sat in the middle of the front row, small and frail like an old blackbird. Pete's ex-wife sat on the end of the same row although her status as family had definitely been revoked. She was wearing a woolly hat that made her seem Russian, even though she was originally from Timaru. She sat and looked bored and after the service she made a point of not talking to any of us. She didn't hang around to chat. Jim joked that she was out of there before the coffin. On reflection, it was probably lucky that they hadn't had any kids.

At the start of the service the minister welcomed Pete's mother and read out a message from Pete's older brother, Tony. It was an email that said that he was working in the Middle East, on an oil tanker in the Persian Gulf, and couldn't get back in time for the funeral. He knew that Pete would've understood.

Looking around, it was clear to us that we were the sum total of Pete's friends. There were a few of his work colleagues, but no one we recognised, and everyone else was family, elderly uncles and aunts and cousins. We sat on the right-hand side of the aisle, which divided the chairs into two groups. Everyone else chose to sit on the left. Al Penny whispered that if it had been a wedding we would have been the groom's whole family. And a strange family we would have been; a loose formation of uneasy middle-aged guys in cheap black suits, barely managing to disguise our shock. You could smell the fear rising off us over the aroma of our musty jackets. As Matt Templeton kept saying over and over again, 'He was only forty-one, forfucksake.' If the Reaper could come knocking at the wrong address like that, what hope was there for the rest of us? That's what we were all thinking as we listened to the minister welcome everyone to Pete's funeral. It scared us shitless.

Pete's coffin was up the front on a metal gurney and the lid was closed. In the last few weeks the cancer had chewed away at him like a bad infestation of borer. Eventually, he forbade any of us to visit the hospice again. He was on strong painkillers, his conversations moved along no track we could follow, and Pete didn't want anyone to see him like that—not even us. In all honesty, we were relieved. The cancer that had at first melted away his fat, making him look younger, had not stopped. It had carried on feeding until Pete was as wizened as a man three times his age. It's hard to see a friend rendered as a living stick-figure. In the end Pete became death's carica-ture.

When he said he didn't want us coming around any more we all went together to say our final goodbye. We crammed into the small private room with its view of the hills. Of course Pete talked about Lucy and the case. The last thing that he said as we were going out the door was to call him if we came up with anything new. Nothing did come up. He died four days later.

At his funeral the minister didn't have a lectern, and spoke standing up the front with his notes in his hands. 'We have come together to remember before God the life of Peter John Marshall, to commend him to God's keeping, to commit his body to be cremated, and to comfort those who mourn with our sympathy and with our love, in the hope we share through the death and resurrection of Jesus Christ.'

We were surprised that Pete had chosen to have the full religious service. Apart from when he was a kid and had attended with his family, we had never known him to go to church. Most of us had also gone as kids, and it was amazing how much of the services we could recall. When the time came, the Lord's Prayer tripped from our tongues as easily as our own phone numbers. When we were asked to respond to the minister's words, we knew just how to speak with that distinctive church rhythm. We felt like children who had been raised in a foreign country and could still fall back into the language when the need arose.

We knew the hymns, which, because we were outside, were sung without accompaniment. There was just the minister leading us on in a shaky tenor voice. We sang along with gusto. We were damned if Pete was going to be farewelled with an apologetic murmur.

> And did the countenance divine
> Shine forth upon our clouded hills?

Once or twice during that particular hymn people swivelled their heads to look at us, nervous smiles stamped on their faces, but the minister didn't seem worried by our braying voices.

> Bring me my bow of burning gold!
> Bring me my arrows of desire!
> Bring me my spear! O clouds, unfold!
> Bring me my chariot of fire!
> I will not cease from mental fight,
> Nor shall my sword sleep in my hand...

After that it was the turn of anyone who wanted to get up and speak. But how do you sum up a friendship you've had your whole life? It didn't seem the right time to be talking about the quest to find Lucy Asher's killer. And so we were left holding a handful of generalities. Those of us who did get up sat down again afraid that we had made Pete sound like every other nice guy whose friends can't quite believe that he's dead.

Out of all of us Roy Moynahan did the best. These days he is a freelance journalist specialising in feature articles, mainly for *North and South* but occasionally for other publications if the money is good. As a writer Roy knew that the details carried the most weight. He spoke about an incident that happened when Pete was in his early thirties, something that most of us had forgotten.

The story went that Pete had been to the movies in town with the woman he was seeing at the time, shortly after he split from his wife, when he saw a guy being attacked on the street.

'The guy was down on the ground and two blokes were laying into him with their fists, and then their feet. So Pete tells the woman he's with to wait where she is. He pulls out a twenty-dollar note from his wallet and hurries over to the two guys. They stop and turn around, ready to take the fight further afield if they have to. Obviously they're thinking that Pete's a friend of the guy on the ground and that he's going to start swinging. But Pete simply holds out the twenty to the nearest guy and says, "I think you dropped this." Pete asks them if they can remember losing the note. One of the guys is quicker than the other and says, sure, he can remember dropping it, "just over there". He points to the ground in the opposite direction to where Pete has come from. "Fair enough," says Pete and hands over the twenty.

'Meanwhile the guy on the ground has seen which way the wind is blowing. He's staggered up, looking no worse for wear than a guy who's been at the bottom of a ruck, although a pretty vigorous one. Quick as, he's limped away and popped into the nearest bar. The two guys had noticed, of course, but didn't seem to care any more. Whatever their issue with him was, it seemed to have been forgotten. They walked away in the opposite direction, laughing.'

As acts of heroism went it didn't seem much, but we were grateful that Roy had resurrected the story and that he had told it well. It struck a tone for remembering Pete that we thought was about right.

Roy finished with a quote from Robert Louis Stevenson. 'Home is the sailor, home from sea/And the hunter home from the hill.' With the cold easterly blustering across the sky and the scream of the gulls clearly audible, we thought that too was about right. 'Goodbye, Pete,' said Roy. 'I hope you know more than us now.' Most of the other people there looked confused but we knew what Roy was on about. He walked back to his seat which, like ours, had begun to sink into the soft spring grass.

After the ceremony, six of us carried the coffin inside and set it down in a mock chapel inside the crematorium. Then we trooped out again, leaving a trail of grass clippings from the damp lawn on the polished wooden floor. There was a final viewing for the immediate family, which, in the absence of Tony, meant his mother.

We stood around in the crematorium's foyer, amid the giant flower arrangements and the soft orchestral music that drifted down on to us from hidden speakers. We talked among ourselves and finished off the last of the sausage rolls and cucumber sandwiches. We knew that at any moment a curtain was going to open behind Pete and the coffin was going to begin its slow journey to the flames. We tried not to think about it.

At first, we didn't recognise the woman who approached Jim. She was no longer skinny but had filled out, as people tend to do in their thirties and forties, although she still had her mother's pale skin and the freckles across the bridge of her nose. Carolyn Asher and Jim each took a glass of juice and went and stood over by the tall windows to talk.

He told us later that she is married now, with three kids, and that her husband is an air-traffic controller out at the airport. Jim showed us a business card. Carolyn owns some type of online company selling merino wool gloves and scarves. Apparently business is good. We agreed with Jim that she looked happy and healthy and all the rest. In fact it had been hard to reconcile our memory of her with the woman standing in the intermittent sunlight coming through the big windows. We had lost track of her when she moved to Auckland at nineteen. By then Carolyn had a police record—she had been heavily into the local drug scene—and the worst reputation of any girl down New Brighton. But, watching her talking to Jim, we had to admit all that was a long time ago. Somehow Carolyn had succeeded in moving on. We wondered how she had done it. What was her secret? When she left, she kissed Jim on the cheek and promised to keep in touch.

We drifted out ourselves soon after. We were almost the last to leave. On the way out we said a final farewell to Pete's mum. She stood by the door looking as though a strong breeze would be enough to knock her over.

When we got back to our homes we couldn't believe that they were unchanged. We've talked about it since and agree that the thing about death that surprises us the most is that, for those who are left behind, the days are essentially unaltered. It seems wrong to eat our dinner at the same table, to brush our teeth with the same brush, to sleep in the same unmade bed as we have always done. There is a disloyalty in the continuation of even mundane tasks. The death of a close friend, and Pete Marshall really was, should be a volcano that blows everything around it apart. But instead, it's a tremor in the night, which barely rattles the cups. It's an earthquake on the other side of a vast ocean, which, if you're not careful, you can sleep right through.

Pete's funeral was on a Thursday. The following weekend there was an All Black test on in the city. A group of us held tickets and, given the price, it seemed silly to waste them. Besides, we didn't feel like hanging around at home, not that week. There was some comfort to be found in each other's company and in the atmosphere of a big game.

It was the second test of the Lions tour and we enjoyed the game, although it won't go down as one of the greatest clashes between the two teams. Since we were teenagers Lancaster Park has been renamed after a corporate sponsor and there is a new stand that rises up on the west side like a sheer wall. It's also true to say that we don't follow rugby like the true believers that we were at fifteen.

These days it's hard to remember just how much stock we put in the game, both the playing and supporting. It seems unbelievable how much it underlined our lives. As we grew up on the Spit, rugby was a natural extension of ourselves, of our fathers, and our neighbours. Rugby has gone professional now and is dominated by the physically superior Maori and Islanders. There are far more games played and the season barely seems to have finished when it is cranked back up. It's hard not to be cynical: not to feel that the game is just another product to be sold and consumed. Rugby is now something for the advertising guys to trade on with carefully packaged appeals to nationalism.

Mark Murray was sitting with us at the Lions game that day. Mark never comes to the games, although he'll sometimes watch them on telly. That day though we had an extra ticket and he'd surprised us all by agreeing to tag along. Mark's wild hair is long gone. It thinned and receded in a sharp

V in his late twenties, to the point where he now allows only the shortest stubble to grow. He sat quietly watching the All Blacks and the Lions, not talking, just staring at the field, where the play ebbed and flowed under the brighter-than-bright lights.

We all understand his reluctance to return to the park. We have lived with the way certain places cause the past and the present to bump uncomfortably up against each other. Mark was here at the first test against the Springboks back in August of '81. He had gone to the game with his father. Mark told us later how he saw the first protesters run on to the field from the embankment. They had to run through the narrow corridors left between the rolls of barbed wire that circled the field. Most of them were nabbed by the police and bundled back over the fence but some got through. About twenty people linked arms on the halfway line and waited for the riot police to arrive, batons drawn.

All around Mark the forty-thousand-strong crowd of mostly men began to bay 'Off! Off! Off!' The guy standing right next to Mark was on his feet, his face beetroot red and swollen with yelling. Mark told us later that he thought the guy might burst. 'I'll never forget what he was saying.'

'Kick them! Kick the commie fuckers!'

Someone else, behind, was yelling 'Kill em Kill em! Kill em!' over and over again until his voice was hoarse.

'I felt sick,' Mark told us later. And then he said something that none of us have ever forgotten. 'It was like being inside the mind of whoever killed Lucy.'

Tug Gardiner was there as well, in a different part of the stadium. He was also with his father. He remembers seeing a policeman punch a protester full in the face. The guy walked up to the cop, hands at his side, and the policeman just drew back his fist and dropped him. Later, as the protesters were herded off the field, there was a deadly rain of bottles and cans, many of them full, from the crowd. One anti-tour guy got hit on the head, the brown bottle shattered, and he fell to the ground like a shot steer at the abattoir. The crowd roared its approval as though the All Black winger had just scored in the corner. Tug looked around and saw that his father was laughing.

Those of us who weren't at the game saw the protests on the *Six O'Clock News.* We watched as the police clashed with the thousands who were throwing themselves in wave after wave at the police defences, trying to get inside the park to stop the game. Blue greatcoats and jabbing batons. Police boots on the wet road. Police lines, riot shields held out front, marching forward into static protesters. Batons smashing down on motorcycle helmets, driven into faces, breaking collar-bones and noses and teeth, shattering eye-sockets. Blood and men and woman of all ages on the ground. It was hard to believe that we were not watching the news from someone else's country. The next day there were pictures in the paper of people lying unconscious on the road. There were black and white images of protesters being led away with broken noses and open wounds on their heads and blood covering their faces.

Over the following weeks we watched the television coverage of all the other games as well. The provincial games in Nelson, Napier, Rotorua, and of course the other two tests in Wellington and Auckland. Through it all we had a growing sense of sadness and unease. We had the feeling that we were witness to something important being broken. It was something we couldn't put a name to but that we had previously taken for granted, and we knew instinctively it could never be fully repaired. As Pete said at the time, 'I suddenly felt like Mum and Dad had told me I was adopted.'

We continued playing and watching rugby after the Springboks returned to South Africa, but something had turned over inside us. Only Jim Turner played beyond high school and then only because his father insisted. Jim's dad still clung to Mr Templeton's belief that if Jim managed to cultivate the right killer instinct then he could go all the way. But after his first season for New Brighton Jim moved away from home and, in the same week, gave away the game for good.

A few days after Pete's funeral, Tug Gardiner got a call from the funeral director. Apparently Mr Marshall had left instructions. His ashes were to go to 'Terrence Gardiner. Do I have the right person?' Tug hadn't been called by his real name in forty years. That was Pete's little joke.

The man from Hayward and Turnbull drove over to Tug's place to personally deliver Pete's ashes. They came in a small, square box that looked like marble but was actually some type of thick plastic. There were no instructions from Pete for what he had wanted done with his ashes, just a standard mention in the will about them being scattered at a place and a time of their recipient's choosing. But that was a no-brainer.

We waited for the weeks to pass. Our lives ticked by after the funeral pretty much unchanged. Every now and then we'd think about the fact that Pete was gone but mostly it felt as though he'd simply decided to take a break and would be rejoining us when he had something new to offer. The days grew longer and the weather eventually warmer, although it was a wet spring. In November the cabbage trees bloomed strongly, just as they had done when we were fifteen. That was supposed to mean a long hot summer. Looking at the halos of white flowers that sprang out from every tree, we couldn't help thinking about Pete's dream, the one where Lucy had looked up at him from beneath the flowering cabbage tree.

Finally the day came. We gathered down on the beach, shortly after dawn, four days before Christmas. The sign warning people about rips and swimming near the channel has long gone. There's a new one further up the beach, closer to the surf club—but despite the constantly shifting sands, we all knew the spot to meet; we could find it blindfolded. The day wasn't going to be as hot as back in 1980, but it was good day nonetheless. There were only a few wisps of high cloud and a gentle on-shore breeze. Jase Harbidge brought along a chillybin of beers and ice, and when we were all there, we cracked the cans open and stood looking at the waves as we drank.

There was a bit of banter and some talk about going for a swim, but no one had their togs. Of course, that led to a few jokes about naked arses and the effects of cold water. Someone brought up the subject of the salty bottles of beer we had once drunk on New Year's. Other memories came out and were passed around.

When the time seemed right, Tug put his empty can down on the sand and took out Pete's ashes from the duffle bag he was carrying. He carefully prised open the lid. We watched in silence. Most of us expected Tug to say a few words and then take out a small handful and toss it gingerly. We thought that maybe he would offer the box around so that we could each take turns at scooping out a bit of the ashes. But Tug simply upended the whole box in one quick movement. The finer ash blew up and swirled back towards the dunes, but most of it scattered on to the beach near our feet, where it quickly became indistinguishable from the sand.

No one had bothered to dress up. We were middle-aged men in shorts and T-shirts. There was a builder and a journalist. A librarian stood next to a guy between jobs who had sold cars for years. A manager of a supermarket stood on the sand shoulder to shoulder with a guy who has a gib-stopping business. There was a cop down from Wellington. We were just normal guys, none of whom would stand out in a crowd. We were locals, down at the beach. Apart from our solemn faces and the empty box Tug held, you wouldn't look twice if you saw us there. We were just a group of men clutching tightly to the past.

Sometimes it is impossible to distinguish between those memories of Lucy that are our own, ones we have actually lived, and those that we have merely gathered together for safe keeping. They shift and move in life's currents.

Lucy on the swings, suspended between the sky and the sandy earth. Just hanging in the air.

Lucy, older now, seen in passing, through the condensation on a car window.

Lucy, waiting with two friends, at the graffitied bus-stop up by the kids' playground.

Lucy in the school grounds at lunchtime, doing nothing much.

There she is in a photograph hung on the wall of a room knee-deep in flowers. She is sitting next to her sister on a park bench. Her father has a protective hand on her shoulder.

We remember Lucy's smiling face flaming into the sky.

Lucy, wearing the red togs she competed in, still with wet sand clinging to her shoulder. She is smiling and holding the trophy out to the photographer like a gift.

Lucy with her hand up in class.

The back of her head glimpsed for a moment amid the wet-day throng in the corridor at school.

Lucy Asher's dry blood smeared on the edge of the silver drinking fountain. The water cascading into the basin catches the sun.

Lucy Asher riding her bike to school on a rainy day. The sky is a concrete ceiling. The hem of her dress is soaked dark, the water coming up off the road in a hissing arc.

Lucy with Carolyn, sunbathing on the wide top step at the school pool. Her hair is wet, fanned out around her head in a dark halo.

Lucy Asher dropping a white paper bag full of Jaffas, which spill and roll across the linoleum floor of the dairy, escaping into the corners and under the shelving like scared mice.

Lucy Asher looking solemn and alone at the front of the class. The teacher's voice drones on about volcanoes.

We remember her picnicking with her mother and sister down on the beach when she was about eight or nine. Her togs were too big for her then and baggy with sea water.

Laughing Lucy behind the counter as she talks on the phone while giving change. Her music is up loud.

Lucy dancing with us in the firelight on New Year's Eve. The light from the flames flushes her cheeks. Her feet are bare on the cool sand.

Lucy ghosting up the right wing, stick in hand, ball at her feet. Now seen. Now lost in the shifting walls of autumn mist.

Lucy Asher's murder was twenty-seven years ago and in another century. It has never been solved. The police still have DNA evidence taken from under one of Lucy' nails, but in the early eighties a DNA database was undreamed of. Even now, when DNA matching has solved Teresa Cormack's murder and the Maureen McKinnel case, plus several other almost forgotten crimes, the sample from Lucy Asher has never been linked to anyone. The police's hard copy of her file sits somewhere gathering dust. Although the case is technically still open and under investigation there's no one in uniform to whom the name Lucy Asher means a thing. Apart, that is, from Grant Webb. He is now a detective and lives up in Wellington. He keeps us informed if there is a case that shows any similarities to Lucy's, or if a likely suspect turns up.

After all these years Al Penny still favours the lone-wolf theory, and in his defence, all of our other suspicions have turned out to be dead ends. Maybe Lucy *was* killed by a stranger who crept in from beyond the borders of the Spit, and just as quickly disappeared off our map. Or, just maybe, the killer has lived among us all these years. Him or him or even him.

Mark Murray did come up with something promising early this year. When scanning the online editions of overseas papers, he found a small article from September 2003. It was about a young woman who had been raped and strangled on a beach in Cyprus, near the port of Limassol. Her attacker has never been caught. She was a nineteen-year-old English tourist from Leeds. The body had been dumped in the sea. The photograph of her which scrolled down on Mark's screen showed an English rose—an almost-chubby redhead. But there were enough similarities to our case to spark Mark's interest and make him print everything out and add it to the files *(Exhibit 135)*.

Limassol is a major sea-port where sailors come and go on every tide. On a whim, Mark got shipping manifests for Limassol for the week that the girl was murdered. They weren't available online and he had to send away to the Cyprus Ports Authority for hard copies and pay an administration fee. When the papers finally turned up in the mail months later, there were pages and pages of tightly packed names of ships, and details of dates and weights, all in columns. Hundreds of ships had come and gone around the time the girl was murdered. Among them, though, was the container ship *Gerd Maersk,* owned by the Maersk shipping company, and registered in Copenhagen. It had berthed in Limassol three days before the girl was murdered and left the morning after. There was nothing strange or suspicious about that in itself and the fact would have gone unnoticed by most people. But Mark Murray is a smart cookie: he remembered that in late 2003, the first mate of the *Gerd Maersk* was Pete Marshall's big brother, Tony.

It's probably the most random of coincidences that brought a man from down the Spit, now working on the other side of the world, close to the scene of another young woman's waveside strangling. As we've discovered over the years, theories are made to be disproved. But as far as theories go, it's an interesting one.

We've grown good at biding our time. We've got our bar and our pool table and our files. We can wait until Tony Marshall berths again in Lyttelton, and then we'll do another interview.

So who killed Lucy Asher?

Despite the thread of hope that Tony Marshall offers, we have to conclude that we may never know for certain. All we do know is that it's impossible for any of us to remember a time before we found Lucy. For better or worse our search for her killer, our search for her, defines us. The case, and everything connected to it, has become as familiar and real to us as our own hand, leg or eye. In fact, it is more real, because it is closer to our core. Certainly, it will be harder to remove should it turn out in the final reckoning to be, like poor old Pete's balls, cancerous.

Since Pete's funeral, Jim and Al have stopped meeting with the rest of us. Tug Gardiner has sold his parents' house and has moved out to the western suburbs. He now lives in a new brick and plaster place in a subdivision of almost identical houses. We helped him shift the little furniture he chose to keep into a rented truck, and since then we haven't seen much of him either. He claims that he doesn't miss the Spit.

Whether any of us can truly put our shared history behind us for good is questionable. We suspect that Jim and Al and Tug will be back, given time. Perhaps they don't really have any choice in the matter. Perhaps we are like the dolls that Lucy's father launched out into the Pacific: always sailing at the whim of the tides and the prevailing winds, course and purpose only an illusion.

Our files of evidence are bulging and our shelves sag, but in the early morning hours when we can't sleep, or during one of those endless Sunday afternoons when it's overcast and raining outside and there's nothing on the box, doubts inevitably bubble to the surface of our minds. As we drive yet again from our homes to the lock-up, we can't help but wonder if we're just wasting our time. On the bad days we are filled with doubt. Then it seems entirely possible to us that our own lives are adrift—that we have spent the best years searching, and yet have gone nowhere that we planned, and know nothing for certain. As the lights of the lock-up flicker back on, and we move to relight the candle beneath the photograph of a smiling Lucy Asher, we sometimes find it hard to hold on to our faith.

fish'n'chip shop song

AND OTHER STORIES

Having won prizes in major national competitions for four of these stories, had several selected for anthologies of significant New Zealand writing, with numerous broadcast on radio and one even translated into Mandarin, Carl Nixon was long overdue for a book of his own, collecting his stories together. So, here they are. Stories that evoke the South Island landscape as well as the New Zealand urban expanse. Stories that take surprising turns as they explore such things as 'saving' a pet parrot, a fruiterer's true love, a return to Crete, an anticipated seduction and the dreams of a suburban mercenary. There are characters to charm and alarm the reader, characters that are startlingly different and characters that are just like us. There are songs of love and tales of loss, there's humour and there's poignancy. Each beautifully told story resonates with a moving depth of emotional understanding.

'With no flamboyance, but with talent and a scrupulous art, Carl Nixon establishes himself as one of our best younger writers'

—Owen Marshal

Made in United States
Orlando, FL
15 April 2022

16860363R00135